The Rejected Wolf

Blue Moon Book 1

Alexa Phoenix

Copyright © 2020 Alexa Phoenix

All rights reserved

The characters and events portrayed in this book are fictitious. Any similarity to real persons, living or dead, is coincidental and not intended by the author.

No part of this book may be reproduced, or stored in a retrieval system, or transmitted in any form or by any means, electronic, mechanical, photocopying, recording, or otherwise, without express written permission of the publisher.

Chapter 1
Andy POV

So, my life somehow got worse...
The fact that I turned 18 last week means I'm now old enough to find my mate. I have been looking forward to this since I was seven years old. When my wolf started going crazy as I was walking out of class, I was unable to contain my excitement. Then suddenly, all I could smell was mint, it was the most amazing thing I've ever smelt. The scent led me out of the building behind the school where I saw him. My mate.

"Fuck" I said as he finally saw me, anger and desire filling his eyes.

Just my luck, it had to be Connor Black.

"It can't be you." He growled at me. I just stood there in shock. How could I be mated to him? He's an arsehole!

Mate!!! My wolf purred in my head.

It can't be him I reasoned with myself, *he's made our life hell for years...*

Mate! She purred again.

It was easy to see her attraction to him, and for a moment I got lost in it. I lost myself in him, in those

dark brown eyes that seemed to try to undress me. As I stared at his 6-foot frame of muscle and a face that resembled a sculpture, I allowed myself to look at him for the first time. While still staring at me, he ran his hand through his jet-black hair, causing his shirt to lift up, giving me a glimpse of his six-pack.
What am I doing???
You're eyeing up our mate, don't worry doll it's natural. He is a hell of a specimen.
I can't like him! I hate him! I responded to her.
Not anymore you don't doll. She purred in response.
"Are you listening to me?" he yelled, interrupting my silent conversation.
"It's Amy, right? Hello?" he said, sounding calmer now.
Does he think my name is Amy? He's ruined my life for years and doesn't even know my name… It broke my heart to think that I meant so little to him.
"I'm sorry, but I cannot do this. There must have been a mistake, there's no way I could have mated with someone like you." His voice was filled with pity.
I felt as though I couldn't breathe, like my world was crumbling under me. He was going to reject me! My wolf howled in agony.
My head turned as I heard Tyler's voice from the car park. "Connor baby? Where are you?"
"I'm coming." Connor yelled back, getting up. With one final look at me he left.
As I sank to the hard floor, I couldn't believe it; I finally met my soul mate, and he was going to reject

me. First time since my parents' deaths, I cried.

Chapter 2

Logan POV

The sound of someone crying stopped me as I walked out of the school grounds. Following the sound, I found her hugging a wall in one of the school buildings. My heart simply broke for the girl as I watched her with her head bowed and her knees trembling in tears.

As soon as she heard me approaching, she became tense.

"Just leave me alone." She shouted out.

I responded without thinking. "I can't do that; I have a rule against pretty girls crying." She seemed to relax at my voice.

"I'm sorry," she said, looking at me. "I thought you were someone else."

I did not say anything, I was shocked. She was beautiful. Nothing like the she wolves around here. Their clothes were too slutty, and they were too heavily covered in fake tan for my taste. She had blonde hair in a mess of curls that flowed down her back. She wore simple clothes, as if she were trying to blend in, though I have no idea how a girl like this could blend in. When her eyes caught mine, I realised they were a beautiful shade of blue. For a second, I even thought they flickered like flames.

I realized that I was staring at the poor girl, so I shook my head and sat beside her.

"What happened to make you so sad that you'd hid away back here?" I asked her.

"You don't have to be nice to me, I'm fine really." I just stared at her waiting for her to answer my question.

She gave a defeated sigh "I found my mate."

I have no idea why, but that one sentence brought me great sadness.

"Was he ugly?" I joked. I was rewarded with the slightest smile.

"No. But he's going to reject me. He started to but got interrupted by his girlfriend." She whispered staring at her feet.

"Why the hell would someone reject you?" slipped from my mouth before I could stop myself.

Why the hell would someone reject this girl?

"He said that he couldn't be with someone like me." She looked defeated as she spoke. I felt an unexplainable sense of rage, causing me to growl as I spoke.

"What do you mean someone like you?"

As she looked directly at me, she said, "He meant to say I wasn't good enough for him, that I am a freak."

Before I could respond a boy ran up to us.

"Andy there you are. Where have you been? I've been looking everywhere for..." he seemed to pause as he saw me and her. "What the hell is going on? Andy are you okay?"

"Alexi I'm fine, let's go we are going to be late." She looked at me as she stood up. "Thank you, for helping me." She said and she walked away with the boy.

Chapter 3

Andy POV

Alexi drove home in silence; I could feel him staring at me worriedly, but I couldn't bring myself to talk. We spent over an hour getting ready for the party tonight at the pack house. The alpha and Luna were welcoming their oldest son (our future alpha) back from university. They invited everyone higher up in the pack to celebrate with them. Our father being a beta meant we were at the top of the list along with our parents. I wouldn't normally attend any pack event, but Alexi had begged me for weeks until I agreed. As we were getting ready, I filled Alexi in on the day's events from finding Connor to the stranger who had helped me. To say he was furious would be an understatement. It took a lot of convincing to stopped him from running to the pack house to attack Connor.

"How are you so okay little sister?" he asked me once he calmed down.

"I'm honestly not too sure. The stranger helped a lot, I guess." I replied as we walked down to find our parents waiting for us.

"Time to go kids. You both look amazing! You

ready?" our mother said walking, over to us.

We both nodded and made our way to the party by car, which took only a few minutes. When we arrived, Alexi held his arm out to me smiling. "Ready to go little sister?"

I took his arm and nodded as we walked into the pack house. The house itself was beautiful. It was on a cliff with an amazing view of the Cornwall beaches below us. The Luna went all out for the party and as we stepped inside, I saw the great hall was decorated in the blues and greys of our pack's crest. There was a band playing calming music whilst people waltzed on the dance floor. I could see the Alpha and Luna leading the dancing couples. The Luna was laughing happily as her gown flowed around her feet.

"I hear the Alphas son hasn't found his mate yet. Which is rather strange as he's like, twenty-two?" Alexi said, pulling me towards the dance floor.

"Alexi, you know I don't dance." I argued trying to pull away.

"Just for tonight, little sister, please?" he gave me the best puppy dog eyes he could until I caved and followed him.

After the first dance I have to admit I started to enjoy myself. I felt elegant watching as my dress swayed with me as I moved.

I was giggling like a child when I heard a growl from behind me. As soon as I turned to see Conner looking directly at me, I ran. His eyes showed pure anger.

I could hear Alexi chasing after me yelling for me to stop but I couldn't. I needed to be outside. I needed air; I couldn't breathe.

When I reached the garden outside the pack house I stopped and felt Alexi bump into me obviously not stopping soon enough.

"Andy are you okay? What happened in..." he didn't get a chance to finish as Connor ran up and tackled him to the ground.

"How dare you, you stupid mutt. How dare you touch what isn't yours." Connor yelled as his fists impacted Alexi's face.

I tried to pull them apart, but Connor pushed me away, throwing me against a tree. I hit it with a deafening thud, pain shot down my back like lightning. I tried to get up and stop Connor before he killed Alexi. Before I could get up, I heard growling coming from my side and I saw him lunge at Connor with fury lighting up his eyes. If I hadn't met the man earlier, he probably would have terrified me with just that one expression.

The stranger easily separated Conner from Alexi and threw him to the ground.

"What the hell is wrong with you Connor?" he yelled.

"Shut up brother, this has nothing to do with you." He growled back.

Wait brother??? As in the future Alpha? Well, I didn't see that coming, I thought, as this stranger started towards me.

"Are you okay? Are you hurt?" he asked, putting his hand on my arm to help me up. At the contact I heard Connor growl again. What the hell was his problem?

"I'm okay. Thank you for helping me again." I replied smiling up at him.

"That's it! I'm done with this" Conner yelled as he grabbed my arm pulling me away. I felt strange sparks at the touch, it gave me chills, but I was too furious to think about that.

"Get your hands off of me." I yelled as I pulled my arm away. I rushed over to Alexi, examining his wounds.

"I'm okay little sister, I'll heal. How're you?" he asked as I bent down. He reached up and brushed a tear away from my cheek.

"Bitch, you are coming with me." Connor yelled. I turned to see my stranger ready to pounce again, but I wasn't taking it this time. He was really starting to piss me off.

"Shut the hell up Connor, you don't get to order me around. You're rejecting me, remember?" I started to make my way towards him, still yelling as I walked. "even if you weren't you had no right to attack my brother. He did nothing to you."

"Brother?" he said, staring at me.

"Yes brother, now just leave me alone."

"No. I won't do that, you need to come with me, you shouldn't have come here. I told you I didn't want you." He said, trying to grab my arm again.

"I came because I was invited, you idiot, my decision had nothing to do with you. Why the hell would you even cross my mind? You've been hell bent on ruining my life for years and rejecting me. Why would I care what you think?" I screamed at him. I saw him flinch at my words.

"Amy, you are being ridiculous." He scowled at me.

That's it.

"My name is Andy you stupid dickhead. You've known me for years and you didn't bother to learn my name." And with that I walked away. My adrenaline drained away, and I began to wobble. Damn I must have hit my head on the tree. I began to fall, but just before I hit the ground, someone caught me. Then the world went black.

Chapter 4
Logan POV

Despite the pack house being filled with wolves, I ignored them. I was looking for her. I couldn't get her off my mind since we met at the school. I was hoping that she would be here, but with the rejection maybe she wasn't going to show. Having given up all hope, I caught her in the corner of my eye looking stunning. Her curls were tamed and spilling down her bare back. She looked breath-taking. She was dancing with the boy from earlier, laughing as he moved her around the dance floor. I wanted to dance with her, hold her as he did. I started walking toward them when I heard someone growl. But my attention was still on her and she looked terrified. And then she ran.

I tried to follow her and the boy, but I lost them in the crowd. Searching, I finally caught her scent and followed it to the garden. As I walked up to them, I saw Connor. He was on top of the boy. The girl Andy tried to pull him off, but he hit her straight in the chest sending her flying towards a tree. I heard the thud as she collided with it, I growled at my brother and went straight for him.

I had him pinned when he started yelling at the girl. She wasn't looking at him though, she was looking at me. Her eyes were filled with confusion. I went to her and helped her up. Checking to see how badly she was hurt when I heard my brother growl again. He was starting to get on my nerves. He started to grab the girl, before I could pull him off, she beat me to it. She ran to the boy and knelt beside him. Was he her mate? He didn't appear to be rejecting her.

I saw Connor advancing on her again and readied myself to defend her when she started yelling at him. I could tell she had been pushed past her limit.

"Shut the hell up Connor, you don't get to order me around. You're rejecting me, remember?" "even if you weren't you had no right to attack my brother. He did nothing to you."

Wait, she's Connor's mate? How in the hell did he get her? And why the hell is he rejecting her.

Connor started to yell back at her, but she just cut him off.

"My name is Andy you stupid dickhead. You've known me for years and you didn't bother to learn my name." For some reason I felt such pride at her. She not only put my brother in his place, but she was so strong. She has been rejected and thrown across the garden and she wasn't showing any weakness. It was impressive. It was hot.

While watching her walk away, I decided to follow her to make sure she was okay. When I caught up with her, she was falling, but I was fast and caught her before her head hit the stone.

When I had placed her on my bed in my room, I walked to grab the pack doctor who was at the party downstairs.

When the doctor came out of my room, he came over to me and said, "She's going to be okay, she hit her head, but I don't think she has a concussion, with all of the stress of the day I think her body just needs rest." I thanked him as he left.

Before going into the room again I mind linked Alexi.

Your sister is doing okay. I have had a pack doctor check on her. It didn't take long for him to reply.

Thank you, Alpha, where is she?

She's safe in the pack house, I will keep her safe until she wakes.

Thank you, Alpha. He responded and then I cut off the link and went inside the room.

# Chapter 5

Andy POV

I woke up to the most amazing view. There was a floor-to-ceiling wall of windows that let me see the beach below. I lay there watching the waves mesmerized. I was so distracted that it took me a few minutes to realize I wasn't home. When I looked around the massive room, I found him asleep across from the bed on a couch. This was the first time I actually got to see him. He was gorgeous, he was muscled, but he was not lean like his brother. He was massive, he appeared to be built like a tank.

As I watched him sleep, he looked so peaceful. His sandy blonde hair was messy and clinging tightly to his face, and his arms were draped across his chest. I would have been delighted to wake up in his room if the circumstances were different. Who am I kidding, circumstances be damned I was still delighted. After getting up, I surveyed the room. It was amazing; the walls were a lovely shade of grey that gleamed in the sun. On one of the walls were weapons, swords, daggers, and a beautiful shield with our pack's crest on it. Two wolves howling at a blue moon. However, the thing that caught my eye was on the other side of the room, there was a wall of books. They lined bookcases ten foot high. I could not resist, walking over to the books I traced my fingers along the spines as I read each one. I was so absorbed in the books I did not hear when my stranger awoke.

"Anything catch your eye?" he asked, coming up behind me.

I jumped at his voice and let out a girly yelp.

Dear God, kill me. I am pathetic.

"I'm sorry, I didn't mean to scare you." he said, and I heard the smile in his voice. I could feel his breath on the back of my neck. He was so close to me.

"you didn't scare me sir." I lied.

"Well, that's good then. How are you feeling?"

"I feel much better, thanks for helping me again." I replied, turning to face him.

"it was my pleasure. I had some of the omegas find you a change of clothes if you would like to wash up?" he gestured towards a pile of clothing beside the bed.

"That's very generous of you alpha, thank you."

"Please call me Logan." He smiled at me.

"Logan it is then, I'm Andy by the way" I said, sounding a lot more confident than I felt.

"It's nice to finally meet you properly Andy".

I grabbed the clothes and showered, my gown was covered in mud, so I folded it up and placed it aside. Dressing in the clothes he had given me. I was grateful that they were rather plain. Just a pair of shorts, a t-shirt and trainers.

When I was done, I walked back out into the bedroom to find my stran... Logan sitting on the bed smiling up at me.

"Feel better?" he asked me but before I could answer there was a knock on the door.

When the door opened it revealed an apologetic omega.

"Sorry Alpha but your father asked me to remind you of the training event today." He said standing in the doorway.

"Yes, I forgot about that, thank you, tell my father I will be there after breakfast." Logan replied.

When the omega left Logan turned to me again.

"Are you hungry?" He asked.

"I'm starving." I confessed.

"Okay," he said, smiling at me. "We'll get breakfast after I get dressed."

I nodded and waited for him. About fifteen minutes later, we were walking to the dining hall. After sitting down and ordering food, he looked at me again, with a look that I could not figure out.

As we ate, he started talking. "so, what is your plan today?"

He asked to make conversation. I thought about it before I replied "Honestly nothing. Alexi and my father are going to the fighting events, so I guess I'm on my own."

"If you are not doing anything you could come to the games? I'm sure it would make it a lot more interesting." He said, staring down at me.

"You don't like fights? I thought today was in your

honour?" I asked him.

"That is why it is uninteresting. I am a spectator today not a fighter." He responded as he finished his meal.

"Will you come?"

"It sounds more exciting than staring at the walls." I joked but I nodded yes.

He smiled at me, making my heart flutter.

We walked to the arena in comfortable silence before being ushered to the best seats in the house. A few minutes later he started explaining the tournament to me, even explaining the fight moves. He seemed to be enjoying explaining it all to me so much that I didn't have the heart to tell him I knew all of it.

"So, there are about 50 wolves competing today. They are showcasing their talents to me for when I take over as alpha. It was all my father's doing."

I nodded and he continued.

"The wolves are paired up in one-on-one fights, and then the winners are paired up and so on until one wolf remains."

"Do you have any bets going?" I teased him.

"No, though my brother is determined to win." I flinched at the mention of Connor causing Logan to look guiltily at me.

"Sorry Andy, I didn't even think. Are you okay?" he looked so apologetic that I instantly said I was fine to ease his conscience.

"I'm up next little sister, you're going to watch right?" Alexi asked as he approached us.

Logan spoke up. "of course, we will be watching."
Alexi bowed to Logan and then looked at me, his eyes full of questions.

Are you two dating? When did that happen? He mind linked me.

We are not dating; he's just being nice. He feels sorry for me because of Connor that's all.

Yeah sure...

The trainer who was running the tournament called Alexi up into the arena saving me from this conversation.

Good luck! I linked him as he walked away.

Alexi was an amazing fighter; he was the son of a beta meaning that he had more strength than most wolves except the alphas of course. His opponent was a massive man though, he stood six feet tall and seemed to be built like a brick wall. They looked like polar opposites, Alexi stood at almost the same height, but his build was smaller. The big tank of a man lunged at Alexi; I could tell easily that he didn't have much elegance to his fighting. I guessed that he probably just assumed his size and strength would make it pointless... he was wrong. Alexi easily dodged every blow thrown at him and knocked him out the minute his fist connected with the man. I had to hide a giggle with a cough as he hit the ground with a thud, a very confused expression on his face.

"Impressive." Logan said beside me.

Given that Alexi was to take over as beta when Logan became alpha, I was glad he seemed to like Alexi.

That's when my father walked over giving me a sad look I didn't understand.

"Sorry sweetie, but alpha black requested it." He said to me.

"Requested wh..." I didn't get a chance to finish because I heard the announcement.

"Andrea Hale, please come to the arena."

I just sat there in shock.

Andy! You have to go up now... Alexi mind linked.

I just shook my head. I hated being the centre of attention. I didn't want to do this, I just wanted to blend in until school was done and then I could leave.

"You have to go up honey." My father said, grabbing my arm to get me to move.

I sighed and stood up to walk down to the arena. I had no way out of this.

Chapter 6
Logan POV

To say I was shocked when the announcement for Andy came over the speakers would be an understatement for two reasons.

One, I had no idea her name was actually Andrea nor that she had a different last name to beta Jackson which confused me.

Two, why was she called up to fight, she's tiny??? Maybe not in height, she stood at about 5,10 but she looked like she weighs nothing...

Watching her walk up to the arena, she looked terrified, and as she tried to calm herself, I saw her eyes widen in shock. I saw why when I followed her eye line. Connor walked out onto the sand looking like he was prepared to tear someone's head off. She was matched up to fight Connor. What were they thinking! He's the son of an alpha, he's got twice the strength of a regular wolf...

As the fight began, Connor lunged at her and she stood motionless.

Crack...

He'd punch her in the ribs causing her to gasp and fall to the floor.

"Get up! Stop being so damn afraid Rea!" I heard Alexi yell from the side-lines, I started getting up to stop the fight when I saw her face. She was pissed but not at Connor, she was pissed at Alexi. She growled at him, but he just yelled again.

"Get up! Right now, Rea! Stop being such a coward!" When Andy got up, I realized he wasn't being a jerk. He was trying to protect his sister before Connor killed her.

Connor came at her again but this time she dodged out of the way causing him to stumble.

He growled and spun around to face her. He hit again and again but each time she just moved out of the way... how was she doing this.

After a few minutes she stopped and stared at Connor daring him to hit her again.

He obliged but just before his hand connected with her face, she moved so fast that the next thing I saw was Connor being thrown and landing next to her. She walked over and grabbed his arm, twisting it behind him, with her foot pressed to his neck. He was pinned. The trainer came back counting to ten. And announced Andy as the winner.

The whole arena was silent. Andy just let go of Connor, stepping on him as she walked out of the arena and sat back in her seat. Everyone just stared at her in stunned silence, don't get me wrong it's nothing to do with the fact she's a girl we have women warriors though not many most she wolves preferred to do other things. It was the fact she defeated an alpha without even breaking a sweat.

Then the whole arena erupted in cheers, it was no secret that every pack member disliked Connor well apart from the young she-wolves who followed him like lovesick pups. He was a dick. How did he end up with her? What was the moon goddess thinking? I was so wrapped up in my inner monologue that I didn't notice Connor running through the crowd straight at her. I managed to catch him at the last second. Stopping him from tackling her.

"What's the meaning of this? My father yelled with all the power of an alpha, making everyone around us run off terrified.

"This damp bitch shouldn't be here!" Connor yelled, turning towards our father.

"You hold your tongue boy!" came from Beta Jackson.

"I won't, she cheated. She must have cheated. She's nothing. She's a dirty rogue."

"Shut the hell up Connor. She beat you. Just accept it." I growled at him. He tried to break free of my hold but was unsuccessful.

"The Goddess made a mistake. I could never be with anyone like you." He glared at Andy.

I saw her flinch away from him.

"What do you mean the Goddess?" my father asked.

The betas eyes darted between Connor and Andy and I saw it click.

"She made that thing my mate!" Connor yelled.

"Mate?" my father said in disbelief. "are you telling me you found your mate, and this is how you choose to treat this gift?"

"I don't want this gift; she can have it back."

I watch Andy turn around and leave. When I looked up to my father, he just nodded at me. I released Connor and went after her.

"Andy!" I yelled chasing after her.

When I reached the door of the arena, I stepped outside looking for her, but she was nowhere in sight. After ten minutes of looking, I gave up and went back to my father.

Immediately after the tournament ended, my father called us into his office. Beta Jackson, Connor, and I walked into the double doors at the same time.

"Good you're all here. We need to discuss what happened." My father told us as we sat down.

"I believe you are the right alpha. I had no idea my daughter had found her mate."

"Connor, why didn't you tell us?" my mother said as she came into the office.

"Because there's nothing to tell. I'm rejecting her anyway."

My parents' faces looked shocked and disappointed, and the beta just growled at Connor.

"Why on earth would you reject Andrea? She's a lovely girl?" my mother asked.

"Because she's a freak. I refused to be with someone like that."

"You think before you speak, boy. That's my daughter you speak of." Beta Jackson looked about ready to rip Connor apart.

"I don't understand how we went so wrong with you." My father spoke up. His face just looked blank.

Conner just growled at him and stormed out of the room.

"Why does he hate her so much?" I didn't realise I had spoken aloud until Alexi responded. When did he enter the room?

"He's always hated her. When she joined the pack he just wouldn't except It." He told me looking sad for his sister.

"What do you mean joined? She's your sister? She was born here." I asked them confused.

Jackson just shook his head at me and said. "My daughter is adopted, she was orphaned when she was young, we took her in." I just stared at him.

"What happened to her family?" I asked him.

"Me and your father went to visit with the crescent moon pack many years ago. There alpha requested us, some of his elders had informed him of a seer who had told him his child's future. He told us that his daughter was destined to join our packs. The seer had told him that she saw the girl with her mate. All the woman could tell was that it was a son of our alpha." He stared at me as he spoke.

"We all thought it would be you." My father said behind me.

Me? Why me?

"So, we travelled to the pack to meet the alpha and his daughter, when we arrived the pack house was in flames. Hunters had gotten to the whole pack, there were no survivors." He sighed. "When we had gotten the flames out, we started searching for any clues to help us find the hunters. I went to the alphas suit.

I found nothing there except the Alpha and Luna were lying on the floor dead. I went to leave, and I heard crying. I found her hiding under the bed, they had died protecting their daughter."

I could see Alexi was trying to appear unfazed, but his eyes were wet as the beta spoke.

"We brought her back and she came to stay with my wife and me. She took an instant liking to Alexi and so we adopted her." The beta finished.

I just sat there taking it all in. I thought Andy was impressive before but even more so now. She had survived the death of her whole pack and was still able to be so kind.

"We always assumed she was meant to be your mate, so when you turned eighteen and didn't find your mate, we weren't worried about you. Because we knew Andrea wasn't eighteen yet." My father told me.

"But it wasn't me. It was Connor."

"Yes, it was. The poor girl." My mother said.

"We have no idea why, but fate decided it would be him."

Chapter 7

Andy POV

I ran as fast as I could, I was so angry and embarrassed that I couldn't control it and I shifted. As I ran, the sand underneath my paws looked like a sandstorm.

I was already the pack freak. Now they all know he's rejecting me.

Andy, are you alright? Where are you? Alexi's voice barged into my head.

I'm fine, I just need some time alone. Then I shut down the connection and blocked him out.

I got back home and shifted before running inside. Being naked in public wasn't on my agenda for today. I have already been humiliated enough; I don't think I could handle anymore.

After showering and changing into some comfortable clothes, I went downstairs in search of food. By food I mean ice cream and chocolate, screw the calories I needed comfort food. So much comfort food.

Just as I removed the tub from the freezer, I felt an excruciating pain in the back of my head and fell to the floor.

Someone had hit me. I could hear them laugh but I couldn't open my eyes. Why can't I open my eyes?

"Not so tough now are you, slut." Somebody smirked at me and everyone laughed.

I doubled over as one of them kicked my stomach, the others held me down and they all kept kicking me. I managed to get one of my legs free, kicking the only one I could reach. My foot caused a horrendous crack to reverberate throughout the room, causing the receiver to growl.

"You dumb bitch, you're going to pay for that". I felt myself slipping away and knew I was going to pass out. They were going to kill me. So, I did the last thing I thought I'd do.

Logan, hel... I didn't get to finish because one of them kicked my head and the world went black.

Chapter 8

Logan POV

Trying to wrap my head around everything, I walked to my room. Was she supposed to be mine? If I hadn't left if I had stayed in town. If I hadn't been so stupid, why did I leave. And then I heard it.

Logan hel... My heart pounded as I sensed her fear. I felt my wolf howl in my head.

I did not think I just ran. I knew where the beta lived, I just had to hope she was at home. The moment I reached the door, I could smell blood a lot of blood. Splitting the door in half, I went straight through it. I didn't care about the damage, I just wanted to get to her. Please be okay, please.

As soon as I saw her I was filled with panic. Her body was completely still, with so much blood, and I was sure she was dead. Her body looked so broken. I knelt beside her and picked up her head, placing it in my lap. I felt tears streaming down my face, but I didn't care. She was dead. I had lost her before I even got a chance to know her. Then she moved, just slightly, and said a word that made my heart leap.

"Logan." Her eyes were swollen shut and I don't

think she knew I was here, but she called out for me. She called for me. Standing up I carried her as carefully as I could to the pack hospital.

After I arrived, the doctors began to run towards us, and I had to place her on a bed while they got to work. I didn't want to let go of her, how could I let her go?

"Alpha what happened to her?" one of them asked me.

I replied, my voice breaking, "I have no idea she was like that when I arrived."

Eventually I was told to leave as they started to undress her to get to the rest of her wounds. I didn't want to leave her, but I obliged and went to the waiting room. My heart ached, and everything inside of me wanted to run to her side. Instead, I decided to contact my father, I needed a distraction.

Father! Someone attacked Andy.

What? Is she okay? My father responded almost instantly.

I don't know. I got her to the pack hospital but it's bad.

I'm on my way, I'll inform Sam. He said and I cut of the connection and waited.

It wasn't long before the waiting room filled up, Andy's parents and Alexi were here within minutes. Mrs Jackson was in tears as her mate held her up, Alexi headed straight for me.

"What the hell happened?" My wolf didn't like anyone demanding something of us, being an alpha meant he didn't take any disrespect. However, I knew he was just worried about his sister.

"I don't know, she was on the floor when I got there. Someone attacked her." I confessed. I saw my mother and father enter the waiting room, my mother going straight to Mrs Jackson. My father looked at us, his eyes looked almost defeated.

"I sent some warriors to look in your house to see what they could find. They found that at least four members of the pack broke in but did not steal anything. They came for Andy."

Beta Jackson let out an enraged growl, causing all of us to flinch. My father put his arm around his friend, trying to keep him calm. We all spent what felt like hours waiting, until one of the doctors came over to us.

"She's stable, but her wounds are serious, she has multiple broken ribs, a fractured skull, a severe concussion and a punctured lung. Her wolf is trying to heal her, but I think it's exhausted."

"But she's going to be alright?" I asked.

"Yes, she's going to be in tremendous pain and will most likely heal slowly but she will live."

"Can we see her?" Mrs Jackson asked.

"Yes, just make sure not to wake her. She needs rest."

I watched them walk into the room, wishing I could go with them. They're her family, so I restrained myself, because I was nothing to her. After a while of sitting in silence I felt a hand on my shoulder, I looked up to see a worried Alexi.

"You are welcome to go into the room, we're going to

take my mother home." Giving him a grateful hug, I entered the room, grabbed Andy's hand, and sat down in a chair next to the bed. My body was already asleep before I realized it.

Chapter 9

Andy POV

It was as though I'd been run over by a dump truck when I awoke. My chest hurt and my breath made me want to scream. I opened my eyes to see the IV in my arm and the monitors connected to me. I was in a hospital bed. I couldn't see much in the room since it was dark except for the blinking light on the monitor beside me, but I felt someone moving next to me, and when I looked up, I saw he was holding my hand. I knew it was a man from the size of his hands, they made mine look tiny. I tried to take my hand away, but he just gripped harder. I knew my pulling had made him wake up though because I felt him move again.

"Andy? Are you awake?" Logan? What was he doing here?

"Hello." My voice came out as more of a croak, but he heard me.

"Thank god. You scared me. Hold on, I'll get you something to drink for your throat." He stood up and walked away. Then a light came on, making me blink.

"Here, drink this." He told me as he handed me

a plastic cup. I drank the water happily; I was so thirsty. When I handed the cup back, I could see his face for the first time. He looked horrible, his eyes looked exhausted, and his hair was a mess.

"Are you okay?" I asked him.

He laughed at me "am I alright? You're the one who was attacked and you're worried about me?"

"You look like hell." I replied, causing him to laugh even harder.

"I'm fine. How are you? Can you tell me who did this to you?"

"I'm okay, just sore, I don't know who it was though. I was getting something out of the freezer, and they hit me on the back of my head. When I fell to the floor, they hit my face and my chest. But I heard them laughing. I think there were three or four of them. I'm sorry. I tried to open my eyes, but I couldn't."

"Don't you dare apologise; you did nothing wrong. Whoever did this is a coward. And I'm going to kill them." He's eyes shone a shade of black and I knew he was serious.

"Thank you, for saving me again."

"It's my pleasure Andy." He smiled at me.

"I'm going to let the doctors know you're awake okay?" I nodded to him and he left the room, a few minutes later Alexi mind linked me.

Andy? Logan said you were awake, are you okay?

Yes, I'm fine.

I was so worried about you little sister. You looked dead. Did you know Logan found you? He broke our front door to get to you. When we got to the hospital, he looked terrified.

Wow he broke our door.

Yeah, it's in pieces. I have no idea how he knew you were hurt though.

Hmm. He was right, how did he know? Then I remembered what I had said before I passed out. I had called for him.

I think I called him before I was knocked out.

You did? Hmm. That guy really likes you Andy.

No, he doesn't, he's just being nice. He's going to be the alpha soon he has to protect the pack.

Nice? He smashed the door! Then slept beside you to make sure you were okay for the second night in a row.

I don't know, maybe you're right but it doesn't matter.

Why not? Don't you like him?

He hasn't found his mate yet Alexi, when he does, he'll forget about me.

Maybe... he sighed.

The door opened and the doctor entered. She was a middle-aged woman with short red hair.

I have to go, the doctors here. I said before shutting the link.

"Hello Miss hale. How are you feeling?" she smiled at me. I instantly relaxed, she just seemed so nice.
"I'm okay, just sore." I told her.
"Well let's have a quick look at you."
She gave me an exam telling me everything I missed whilst I was asleep, then she said I could go home in a few days if I promised not to leave my bed for a while. I agreed eagerly and she left. Not long after I fell back to sleep again.
When I woke up again, the sun was shining through the window, and Logan was sitting in the chair again, staring down at his phone. He looked much more relaxed than he did earlier. His hair was neatly styled, and he was wearing fresh clothes.
What if he likes me? I stopped myself immediately from continuing. Liking him would be a mistake. He hasn't found his mate yet; it would only leave me heartbroken.
I sat up in bed and looked around. I found a bouquet of roses on the table next to me. They were beautiful. I reached over and read the note.

Dear Andrea,

I wasn't sure what flowers you liked but I hope these will do.
You had me worried there, please don't do that again.
Logan x

"Are they okay?" Logan asked me, causing me to jump and then instantly groan at the pain the movement caused.

"They are beautiful, thank you."

"I also got you these, Alexi said you would like them." He handed me a box wrapped in red paper. I tore the paper away and squealed. Chocolate!

"Omg, chocolate, thank you I'm starving." I said as I ate one. It was the most delicious thing I have ever tasted; it was filled with a creamy caramel and I couldn't help the moan that escaped my lips. I instantly blushed when I heard him laugh.

"I take it you like them?"

"I have a slight addiction to chocolate, well to anything sweet really. These are amazing, I've never tasted anything this good. You're going to have to tell me where you got them so I can buy their whole stock." I said shoving two more chocolates in my mouth. Making him laugh again. I really like it when he laughs.

"They're handmade in a cafe in Bude. I'll have to take you sometime. They also do cake, like twenty types of cake actually."

"That sounds like heaven, I'm going to need to live there." I replied.

Before he could reply the doctor came back in. She smiled when she saw me with a mouth full of chocolate.

"Hello Mrs Hale, I was going to ask if you were feeling better but by the looks of it you are." She laughed as she checked my chart.

"Hmm, you seem to be healing a lot faster now, so I don't see any reason to keep you here as long as you stay on bed rest. You wolf is starting to do its job, some of the smaller cuts have already healed." She smiled at me.

"Thank you, I'd love to go home." I told her. She nodded at me and said she'd go grab the paperwork.

I looked over to see a concerned looking Logan.

"Are you okay?" I asked.

"I was thinking maybe you should come to the pack house; we don't know who attacked you. You will be safer there."

I thought about it and he was right of course, I am pretty good in a fight, but I'm injured and there's nothing stopping them from coming whilst I'm asleep.

"You may be right, I'm not sure I would feel safe at home. At least not until I'm healed." I agreed.

I saw him visibly relax. "okay then, I'll get Lex to pack some clothes for you."

By the time we got back to the pack house, it was already late afternoon. I started to get out of the car, but he stopped me.

"What do you think you're doing?" he asked as he walked to my side of the car.

"I'm getting out of the car." I replied confused.

"You almost died, there is no way you're walking." He stated then he reached down and picked me up bridal style causing me to let out a very unattractive yelp.

"I can walk you know?" I protested, but I didn't struggle honestly, I was exhausted.

He just laughed at me and walked inside and carried me upstairs. When we were in his room, he placed me on his bed and sat beside me.

"So, what would you like to do? Until you're healed, I'm your personal slave. So, feel free to order me about. And don't you dare get out of bed."

I couldn't help it. I started laughing, like an actual full belly laugh.

"Did I say something funny Andrea?" he asked looking annoyed which only made me laugh harder.

"You're the alpha, or soon to be anyway. You should be ordering me about not the other way round. And no-one apart from my parents call me Andrea. Everyone calls me Andy." He stayed silent for a minute then replied.

"Well until you are healed, in this room you are the alpha okay. And I like Andrea, it's a nice name." He responded.

"Well okay then, if you say so."

"So, what would you like to do? Do you want to watch a movie?"

"Yeah, a movie sounds good, can it be a horror movie? With snacks?" I asked, getting excited.

He started laughing again "sounds good to me. Why don't you pick the movie and I'll go find some food?" I nodded and he left.

After looking through the Netflix choices I settled on the conjuring and waited for him to come back.

When he walked back in, he was carrying a tray that he placed on the end of bed and then joined me again.

"Ooh nice choice. Okay I got everything sweet I could find. We have toffee popcorn, ben and jerry's fudge ice cream and lots of chocolate. What would you like first?" I swear this man is amazing... Why did he have to be perfect?

"Hmm. Ice cream" he picked up the tub and two spoons and handed me one. And I started the movie. We watched quietly eating the ice cream until one of the ghosts in the movie suddenly jumped at the screen and I felt Logan jump next to me. I was in hysterics, I laughed so hard I was crying.

"You... okay there... alpha..." I said between laughing fits.

He straightened, "I'm fine, you imagined it." He lied. I started laughing again and he just glared at me.

"don't worry, your secrets are safe with me." I joked.

He just grumbled something about how he could take a ghost and we went back to watching the movie.

When it was finished it was already dark outside and I could feel my eyelids drooping. So, I stood up to go to the bathroom, but Logan stopped me. "Where do you think you're going? Your on-bed rest."

I rolled my eyes at him. "I need to shower and change. Can you help me with that alpha?" I said sarcastically. I regretted my words however because his eyes started to darken. It seemed like he was getting up to come with me...

"Don't tempt me, little one. Believe me I would happily join you if you asked." He said in a low incredible sexy voice. I shuddered, damn... it took every bit of self-restraint I had to shake my head and head for the bathroom grabbing my toothbrush and a change of clothes from the bag Alexi had brought over on my way. I could hear him chuckling as I shut the door making sure to lock it.

I showered, brushed my teeth, and got dressed in the only pyjamas I had, I silently cursed Alexi. The outfit he had packed was a silk blue set, mini shorts (might have as well been underwear) and a very thin matching vest top. As I looked at my reflection in the mirror, I could see the massive bruises covering my face, arms and chest. Sighing, I walked back inside the room. Logan turned and stared at me...

"What is it? Do I look bad? I can change." I was rambling because the way he was staring at me was making me feel awkward.

"Nothing's wrong, little one, please don't change. I like it. I like it a lot." He said in that low voice that weakens my knees. I instantly started blushing and just stared at the floor.

He got up and walked towards the bathroom stopping when he was passing me.

He put a finger under my chin and lifted my face up, so I was staring at him. "Do not hide that beautiful face from me, little one." Jesus, I'm not going to make it... I'm doomed, this god like man made of muscle was turning me into a hot drooling mess.

"I'm going to shower, why don't you get in bed, you must be exhausted." He said as he walked towards the bathroom.

When I got to the bed, I collapsed on it. I need to remind myself he's got a mate out there somewhere.

True doll but he is a fine-looking man. My wolf spoke up.

Ugh not you too! He'll break our heart.

Maybe but one excellent night wouldn't be such a bad idea...

True... wait no. I can't. Can I? Maybe... ugh.

Your choice doll, but feel free to suggest a run-in the moonlight...believe me I wont say no...

I instantly blocked her out. Ugh, why did I have to get the wrong brother? I swear the moon goddess is laughing at me.

I gave up and crawled into bed, I was just closing my eyes when I heard the bathroom door open. Turning around I saw Logan walk out soaking wet in just a towel that was tied around his waist. I just stared, he had an eight pack and I swear the towel barely covered the massive appendage hiding beneath. I'm not proud of it but I'm pretty certain I was drooling.

"You okay there little one?" he was staring at me smirking. I just hid my face in the pillow blushing so hard I thought my face was burning.

I could hear him laughing, and then I felt him lie down beside me.

To avoid any more embarrassment, I rolled to the side facing away from him to go to sleep. Luckily for me it didn't take long before I drifted off.

Chapter 10

Logan POV

When I awoke, Andy was lying on top of me. Her lips were pressed up against my chest, and her hair was covering her top half like a blanket. However, her bottom half was exposed, as evidenced by those unbelievably short shorts. Without thinking, I slid my hand down and rested it on her back. As my hand touched her, I sensed she was moving, and thought she was going to wake up.

She moved again and I felt her shift her weight. I turned my head to look at her face and her eyes opened, and she stared at me. Her eyes changed to a bright blue that swirled and flickered like flames. I was too mesmerised by her eyes to remember my arm was around her effectively holding her in place. Her eyes went back to normal and then widened.

"What the hell?" she asked as she crawled off of me.

It was like my whole body wanted her to stay as close to me as possible. Her blush was a gorgeous shade of red and I tried to act as natural as I could.

"Morning Little one. How did you sleep?" she looked over at me and I could see that she was trying not to smile.

"I slept rather well actually, you?"

"Not too bad, though waking up to you straddling me definitely improved my night." I winked at her as she groaned blushing again.

While she spoke, she slapped my arm and said, "I was asleep, I didn't control that." I faked injury "ouch little one that hurt, you're going to pay for that." In a flash I rolled on top of her and with one hand I held her arms above her head and with the other I started tickling her. It was adorable to see her squirm and giggle like crazy.

"Say I win, and I'll stop." I told her as I continued to tickle her.

"Never! I never lose. Anything you do I'll do straight back, only better." She said full of determination. She managed to get one of her hands free and started tickling back.

As I grabbed her hand and placed it next to her head, I said, "I'm impressed, baby."

"Anything I do huh?" I smirked as I leaned down and pressed my lips to hers lightly. I felt her tense up but then she relaxed and stopped trying to get loose. Smiling, I kissed her again only this time it wasn't lightly. My wolf grew mad when she kissed me back, so I released her hands and put one behind her head while pulling her closer. With the other hand, I ran it down her side from her top until I reached underneath and placed it on her chest as she moaned loudly in my mouth. I could feel my wolf trying to come out. I was about to remove her top when the door flew open.

"What the hell are you doing?" Connor yelled at us.

"Fuck off, Connor." I yelled back getting off of Andy.

"What the fuck do you think you're doing with my mate?" his eyes had gone black, and I knew his wolf was trying to come out.

"I said get the hell out." I grabbed his arm to push him out the door.

"Get off of me. I knew she was a dirty little slut. Enjoy my sloppy seconds brother." He spat as he left the room.

I turned around to see Andy packing up her things.

"What are you doing? You're supposed to be in bed. Andy, please calm down, it's okay I'm here with you." She didn't look at me. "I... I can't. I'm sorry, I have to go." I walked over to her and wrapped my arms around her. "You don't have to go anywhere, little one. You can stay here with me. I've never felt like this before, I don't want you to go. I don't want to be away from you, please stay." She turned around in my arms and stared up at me.

"I'm sorry but this can't work." My heart broke and I released her, getting angry.

"Why the hell not? And don't say it's because you don't like me because I know you do; I can feel it. I felt it when you kissed me." She looked on the verge of tears.

"This was a mistake. I can't live with you rejecting me too. I'm sorry, but I just can't." she said as she put on a coat and started to leave.

"I'm not going to reject you Andy. Please don't do this." I pleaded.

"You will. One day you'll find your mate and you'll reject me. I'm sorry Logan, goodbye." She said as she walked through the door.

What the hell just happened? One minute I'm having the best kiss of my life and the next I am alone.

Chapter 11

Andy POV

I walked as fast as I could, my whole body hurt but I needed to get home. I couldn't stay here. Connor stopped me just as I reached the door.

"You think you can get away with this?" he sneered at me.

I can't take this anymore. "Leave me alone Connor. If you're not going to be man enough to reject me then I'll do it. I, Andrea Hale reject you, Connor Black as my mate." I said in a rush. Immediately after saying those words, my heart ached. As Connor staggered back clutching his chest, I held my head high and walked out the door home.

When I got home, I broke down. The weight of everything that just happened was too much for me, and I began to cry.

Alexi came rushing towards me. "Andy? What happened?" I felt his arms go around me, comforting me.

Between sobs, I managed to get out, "I rejected Connor and broke up with Logan." Alexi picked me up in bridal style and carried me upstairs to my room. I was too tired to fight him.

That night, I cried in my brother's arms, missing Logan more than I could even understand.

Next couple of weeks were a blur of tears, chocolate, and Alexi's attempts to cheer me up, but nothing worked. My eyes filled with tears as I tried to forget about Logan, but I couldn't. After a week of self-pity, I got dressed and headed out the door. I wanted to see Logan. Living so close to him was killing me, and I couldn't bear it anymore.

I was about to walk through our front door when my mother's voice stopped me.

"Andrea? Is that you?" I could hear the surprise in her voice. I couldn't blame her. I haven't left my room in over a week.

"Hey mum, I was just leaving." I replied, walking into the kitchen. She was making dinner. Her long red hair was in a messy bun and her baggy trousers were covered in flour from cooking. This look was normal for her; she was never one to care about looking proper or perfect. She always told me that she never trusted anyone who said they enjoyed looking perfect every day.

"I am glad you are feeling better sweetie. This letter was delivered this morning for you."

Once I had the letter, I said my goodbyes and headed for my car, sitting in the driveway and opening my mail.

Dear Miss Hale,

In reviewing your application, I am pleased to offer you a place in our music course here at Manchester

University. This course will start in September, but I would like to offer you a place in our summer program. It may be of interest to you.

Oh My God... I got in. I never thought I would. My top school is offering me a spot at the other side of the country, maybe this is a sign.

I don't know, Doll it's very far from your pack. My Wolf tried to reason.

I know but that's kind of the biggest selling point right now. I replied.

Moving is my best option. So, it's what I'm going to do I thought as I walked back into the house.
The next day I was starting to feel better, the idea of starting fresh somewhere else had given me hope. Hope that I will heal.
"Andy, this is crazy, why can't you just give it a try with Logan? At the very least it will help you get over Connor." Alexi pleaded for the tenth time today.
"I can't Alexi, I just can't take anymore. I'm leaving Cornwall." I finally admitted.
He looked so shocked and confused that I was worried I was going to cry again.
"What do you mean you're leaving?"
"I got into the music program at Manchester. I'm leaving tomorrow after my last exam. They have a summer music course that starts next week so I decided to head there early." I knew I was being unfair and selfish leaving him, but I couldn't be here anymore. I couldn't see Logan or Connor without my

heart breaking more.

"Tomorrow? You can't leave tomorrow! It's the Alpha ceremony. They're announcing Logan as Alpha and me as Beta. I wanted you there." He argued.

"I can't see them, Lex. I love you but I can't. Please understand." I was begging and my eyes were beginning to water again. I was such a mess I needed to get away from here. I could see the battle in his eyes, he wanted me there. He was hurt but he was the perfect brother and knew how hard it would be for me.

"He's a mess you know?" I knew he wasn't talking about Connor. It had to be Logan. "I'm not saying it to be mean I just thought you should know. If you can't come tomorrow, I understand little sister but I'm going to miss the hell out of you." I could see his eyes were glossy with water too as he came and sat next to me wrapping his arms around me.

"I'm going to miss you too Alexi." I spoke between sobs.

I fell asleep in his arms before he left.

My mother cried and hugged me so tightly the next morning that it hurt. My father made sure my car was roadworthy and helped me pack it before he broke into tears. Once everything was packed, I said my last goodbyes and got into my car, shouting good luck to Alexi, he did the same to me for my test, and I headed for the school.

I had decided to leave straight from there so I would make it to Manchester before it was too dark. I appreciated that my test was practical and all I had to

do was perform an original piece of classical music for my teachers. Piano playing has always come naturally to me. I have been playing since before I joined this pack. My mother had taught me when I was young. She used to play for me if I couldn't sleep.
It was a quick, painless exam, and after I got back in the car, I headed out of town.
I stopped before I reached the town border.
"I'm a terrible sister." I cried, sitting in my car. I parked it on the side of the road. I could hear cars passing by me.

No, you're not Doll. My wolf answered me.

But I'm not there. This is the biggest night of his life; we have been talking about it for years.

Then go. Don't let any boy stop you from seeing your brother. You're stronger than that.

"Screw it!" As I made my decision, I headed for the pack house, stopping first to change at the school. I knew the warriors at the party would be under strict orders from the Luna, that it was a black-tie event. No exceptions. So, I put on a cute knee length strapless red dress and heels and headed to the pack house.
When I arrived, I saw all the candles they had placed around the house, it was lovely.
When I entered the building, I heard wolves yelling congratulations. So I knew they had just finished the ceremony. The ballroom was decorated with simple greys and blues, but it just made it look elegant and

regal. The whole place smelled amazing, it smelled like caramel chocolate and roses.

Mate! My wolf howled in my head.

I know, I don't want to see Connor. I replied.

Not him Doll, someone else.

What? Where?

I have another mate. I knew it was a possibility albeit rare it does happen. But usually, it takes years to happen. Not days... who could it be? I walked into the huge room and looked at all the wolves. The smell of chocolate was getting stronger and stronger. I couldn't find anyone, I was about to give up when my eyes looked onto his and without thinking I growled "mine."

Chapter 12

Logan POV

I had been locked in my room for the past two weeks; I was a mess. Every time I tried to mind link Andy, she blocked me out. I tried visiting her house, but Alexi refused to see me. I'm worried about her; I know that they had finally gone through with the rejection. I just wanted to help her, but she won't let me.

My father had to force me to come to this stupid ceremony. I didn't want to have a party but here I am dressed up in a stupid black tux waiting for the ceremony to begin.

"Hey man, how are you doing?" Alexi asked as he ran up to me.

"I've felt better. How's Andy? Is she coming tonight?" I asked hopefully, but my hope was short lived when I saw his expression sadden.

"About Andy, there's something you should know. She's left."

"What? What do you mean left?" I growled at him causing him to shrink back.

"She accepted a place at Manchester. She left a couple hours ago." He told me.

She was really gone. I couldn't believe it.
"I don't understand, why did she have to leave?"
"Because she's a mess, she hasn't left her room in weeks. All she does is cry and sleep. She's trying to find something to make her feel normal again. I hate it too dude, I want my sister, but I understand it. She needs it." He looked so defeated that I put my hand on his shoulder to comfort him.
"I appreciate you telling me Lex." I said honestly.
"You're my friend, I love her, but I had to tell you and I think she would accept that."
The ceremony was finally starting so we walked onto the stage and were greeted by over a hundred wolves cheering. My father went through the motions of the speech and the ceremony, but I wasn't paying any attention. I nodded and said yes to every question he asked until he announced I was the new Alpha, and the crowd went crazy again.

Mate! My wolf howled at me.

What? Here? Where is she? He wasn't answering me, he was just howling in my ear. As I was looking through the crowd, I noticed the best scent I had ever smelt. It smelled like popcorn. I jumped off the stage and started looking through the crowd, ignoring my parent's objections. I had to find her.
My eyes finally landed on her beautiful flaming blue eyes and I growled "Mine". The whole crowd went silent and stared at us.
I couldn't believe it. I couldn't believe I was this lucky, Andy stared at me with the biggest and cutest

smile I had ever seen, and I ran to her. Her laughter was contagious as she laughed at me. I picked her up by the waist and spun her around in the air.

"Hello," she said as I put her on the ground. The crowd started cheering again, but this time it was us they were cheering for.

When "Hi" came out of my mouth, I cupped her face in mine. I kissed her, my mate, my Andy like she was my air.

"Congratulations son." My father said breaking our kiss.

"Welcome to the family Andrea." Came from my mother.

Before I could react, Andy was pulled from my arms and lifted into the air, I started growling at the wolf who dared touch my mate.

"Whoa, calm down there Alpha. I'm not taking my sister from you; I'm just congratulating her." Alexi defended himself. I instantly calmed and smiled at him as he shook my hand. "Welcome to the family brother, good luck. She's a handful." He joked at me. Andy slapped his arm and called him a jerk.

"I am not a handful!" she protested.

"As long as you've got a steady stream of sugar, I suppose you're bearable." She started to slap him again but stopped.

"You jerk, I mean you're right but you're still a jerk."

"If you all don't mind, I'm going to steal my mate now." I grabbed her hand and started pulling her out of the hall.

"Where are we going?" she asked as we rushed out.

"Slow down, do you know how hard it is to run in heels?" I stopped and looked at her. She looked gorgeous, she was wearing a bright red strapless dress that made her chest look damn sexy and red stiletto heels. Giving up I lent down and picked her up bridal style and kept walking. She put her arms around my neck. Anywhere her skin touched mine, sparks spread across my skin, giving me Goosebumps.

"Logan where are we going?" she asked again but I stayed silent and walked towards the cliffs behind the house. I carried her down the path until we reached the beach at the bottom. There was a beautiful sunset over the water, and most of the beach and surrounding forest was owned by the pack. After sitting her down in the sand and tying an arm around her waist, I held her tight, and she hugged me.

"This is my favourite place little one. Do you like it?" I asked nervously.

She smiled up at me and wrapped her arms around my waist. "I love it. It's beautiful." I sighed with relief and put my hand under her chin, lifting her face towards mine. I kissed her. We were both gasping for breath when we disconnected. She sighed and sat up fidgeting with her hands nervously.

"What's wrong little one?" I asked her, starting to get worried. Why did she look scared? We were mates! Was she not happy...?

"I need to tell you something." She looked up at me and I could see the water pooling in her eyes.

"Andy, what's the matter? Are you interested in being my mate? I didn't even think to ask." I pleaded, terrified for the answer. She just stared at me, shocked.

"No, that's not it. I couldn't be happier; I was miserable without you. Alexi thought it was the rejection that broke me, but it wasn't it was you." I sighed with relief and wrapped my arms around her pulling her on my lap.

"Then what is it baby?"

"I'm sure you know about my parents." I nodded to her.

"I know about the seer and that you were fated to end up with us." I told her.

She looked at me confused. "What seer? What are you talking about?" She didn't know. So, I told her everything my father and beta Jackson had told me.

"They knew I'd end up with a black brother. I wonder why my dad's never told me... do you think it was always supposed to be you? Maybe it was because I saw Connor first..." she was rambling. Though it kind of made sense.

"Maybe little one. I don't know but I'm glad you're mine now. If you didn't know about the seer then what is it, you wanted to tell me?"

She started fidgeting with her hands and stared out into the ocean as she spoke. "That's not the whole story, I never told anyone not even Lex, but I know why the Alpha requested they come visit quickly. I was walking with my mother and a hunter jumped out at us. He grabbed my mother and I reacted." She looked at me, her tears escaping her eyes.

Chapter 13

Andy POV

I started fidgeting with my hands and stared out into the ocean as I spoke. "That's not the whole story, I never told anyone not even Lex, but I know why the Alpha requested they come visit quickly. I was walking with my mother and a hunter jumped out at us. He grabbed my mother and I reacted."
"I shifted." I whispered.

10 years ago...

"Rea honey, breakfast is ready." My mother yelled.
"Coming." I yelled back, running downstairs. The smell of pancakes grew stronger as I approached the kitchen. In the kitchen, my mother was standing at the counter with a plate of chocolate chip pancakes, smiling at me as I entered.
"Rea sweetie, can you fetch your father. He's in his office again." I nodded and walked towards my father, knocking on the door impatiently. Nothing, sighing, I went inside. He was sitting at his desk, running a hand through his hair. Something was worrying him; he always does this when he's worried.

It was only then that I noticed the phone in his hand. "She's going to do it; I haven't changed my mind. I told you this all before, I don't understand why you keep bringing it up Michael."

He seemed to realize that he wasn't alone anymore, looking up his eyes met mine and he smiled.

"Goodbye." He said quickly before hanging up the phone.

"When did you get here, kiddo?" he asked as he walked towards me. Staying silent, he picked me up, tickling me so that I giggled.

As I giggled, I said, "Stop, mom said breakfast was ready." He threw me over his shoulder. "Well then, let's not keep her waiting."

Once breakfast was over, my father went straight back to work, my mother cleaned up the table, and I went to my mother's music room. The walls were red, and the room was empty aside from her massive grand piano in the centre of the room, it was my favourite room in the house. When she moved in, my father designed it for her.

My mother interrupted my thoughts, "I thought you'd be in here, shall we have another lesson?"

My mother played the piano with ease and I loved watching her play, so I nodded as she walked to it.

We always took a walk through the pack lands after my lesson. Mom always says that it is essential for the pack to see their Luna and future Alpha, as well as to remember what a part you play in this pack.

Letting go of my mother's hand, I ran through the

trees; a dense forest surrounded us, making it seem like something out of a fantasy. My mother called after me, but I ignored her. I kept running until it started to feel wrong, something wasn't right.

Run! Not stopping to wonder who said that I just ran. Before I reached my mother, I saw a man aiming a gun at her. I ran towards her without thinking, just reacting. Although I felt every bone and muscle in my body shifting, I kept running, leaping before the stranger could shoot his gun.

The man stared at me with terrified eyes before running in the opposite direction. I went to chase him, but my mother held me back, wrapping her arms around me, holding me in place. After a few quiet moments, I heard footsteps coming towards us, immediately tensing up, ready to fight whoever it was.

"Don't worry sweetie, it's okay." my father's voice drifted to me and I calmed down. He knelt down in front of me and reached a hand towards me.

"Can you change back?" tilting my head, I looked at him confused. Before looking down, I was a wolf. That's not possible. You can't shift until you're sixteen. I started to panic, what's happening to me.

"It's okay, just calm down. We are here for you." My father reassured me as he spoke.

I felt my body changing again, slowly my body went back to normal. My father wrapped me in his coat before carrying me back home.

I woke up to find myself in my room, I must have fallen asleep. My whole body hurt. I stood and went to look for my mother. Stopping outside my father's office, I could hear her talking to him.

"Do the elders have any ideas?" my mother asked.

"No, they are just as confused as we are. I called blue moon and told them to join us."

She sounded worried as she said, "You told them what happened."

"No, just what the seer told us, nothing more." he replied.

"Rea, you can come in, kiddo." I tensed, wanting to know how he knew I was here.

When I walked in through the door, my father came towards me, lifting me up into his arms. "You should be resting."

"I'm sorry." I whispered.

He smiled down at me, my mother walked over, kissing my forehead. "You have nothing to apologize for honey."

"Let's get you back to bed." my father spoke as he started to walk towards my room.

After placing me in bed, he kissed my forehead and tucked me in. "Good night Rea, get some sleep. Everything will be okay, promise."

The sound of screaming woke me up, my mother ran into my room, grabbing me and we ran. She pulled me towards her bedroom, her hand gripping mine tightly. My father rushed through the door; he was bleeding. He ran to us, hugging us tightly before speaking. "They're all dead, the hunters came whilst we were sleeping."

My mother's cry's stopped him from continuing, he reached out and caressed her cheek. "We have to run." she whispered.

"There's no time, they have the house surrounded." My parents stared at each other before looking at me. Their eyes glistened with tears.

My mother hugged me and said, "We love you so much."

The sound of footsteps echoed outside our door, and my father rushed me under the bed.

"You have to hide, do not make a sound, do not come out for anyone. Promise me."

The words came out slurred as my voice staggered. "I promise."

I watched them stand in front of the bed with their hands linked, shielding me as the hunter entered the room. He yelled out, "Where is she?" but my parents refused to respond. A hunter shot my mother, my father's agonised howls filled the room. My father lunged at the hunter, but another shot echoed, and I watched my father fall to the ground. He reached his hand out to my mother as he died.

I watched as the hunter began looking for me, flipping over the desk and emptying the wardrobe before turning towards the bed. He smiled and reached for me. When I became terrified, my chest started to burn. It got hotter and hotter, and I screamed. My arm was seized by the hunter, who pulled me out, but his jacket caught on fire. He began screaming in agony and ran out of the room. I heard the other hunters yelling "Fire! The buildings are on fire!" and I stayed hidden under the bed. I stayed under the bed listening for what seemed like hours, as the screaming gradually faded. Then I heard yelling, and I saw someone kneel beside my father and whisper to him.

"I'm sorry old friend." I cried as he put a blanket over them. He must have heard me because he looked at the bed. I watched him carefully as he made his way towards me, when he knelt down next to the bed I flinched away.

"It's okay. I won't hurt you. Your name is Andrea, right? My name is Jonathan." He stayed there waiting for me to move towards him.

"Don't worry, you're coming home with us." He told me as he carried me out of the packhouse.

The present...

We just sat in silence for a few minutes before I finally spoke.

"Do you think I'm a freak? I honestly have no idea how I did it." I whispered.

"No little one, I think you're extraordinary." He wiped the tears from my cheek, and I relaxed in his arms.

"I'm sorry I didn't tell you sooner, but I didn't know how."

"You have nothing to be sorry for Andy." he put his hand under my chin, turning me to face him. "You are perfect as you are, I love you Andrea Hale. You are mine forever, exactly as you are."

Smiling up at him I whispered. "I love you too Logan

Black."

Chapter 14

Andy POV

Last night was the best night of my life, I met my mate and finally told a secret I've held onto for ten years. My perfect night was topped off when Logan told me he loved me! I couldn't believe it. The rest of the night was spent making out in his room... I love my life; I'm with a godlike man who loves me and is currently sound asleep next to me. It feels like I've found my other half.

"What are you thinking about, little one?" Logan sleepily asked, pulling me into a bear hug.

"I was thinking how lucky I was and how your scent was making me hungry." His eyes changed into a black lustful shade as he got on top of me and grabbed my hair pulling me towards him. He always makes me forget everything when he kisses me, and I'm lost in a world of desire for him.

"Hungry huh, little one? What is it you're hungry for?" He asked in that deep voice I love so much.

"Chocolate, specifically those chocolates you gave me in the hospital, they were amazing." I said honestly. Laughing, he stared at me.

"What made you think of those chocolates?"

"That's your scent to me, the smell of those chocolates."

"I suppose I shouldn't be surprised your favourite scent would be chocolate..."

"Technically handsome, it's the chocolate you gave me. What do I smell like to you?" I asked curious.

"Popcorn, specifically the caramel one we had when we watched that ghost movie." He put his nose to my neck and breathed in me, making me shiver.

"Are you sure that's all you're hungry for, little one?" he slid his hand underneath my shirt.

He chucked again and moved his mouth to my neck, running his tongue down my shoulder where his mark would be one day. I couldn't hold back the moan that escaped from my mouth.

"Hmm." How is he so good at making me feel like this? I felt sparks on my skin everywhere he touched me. It was the opposite of painful. My mate, therefore, made anywhere he touched me feel ten times better than anyone else because we were one and the same.

In another breath-taking kiss, his hands reached down to my waist. I used the extra moving space to move us up, so I was positioned on top.

"I'm impressed little one. Just how strong are you?" he chuckled at me. While I was bending down kissing him, I ran my hands through his hair, yanking it. When I stopped kissing him, he growled at me.

"Don't worry handsome, I'm not going anywhere." I told him as I pulled my shirt over my head.

He looked at me, his eyes darken even more.

"You're beautiful Andy."

When I blushed, his grin widened.

"Not that I don't like you straddling me, but I like you better under me." he grabbed me and turned me over as he talked. I kissed him again and moved my hands down to his chest, pulling his shirt over his head.

My breasts were first kissed before he kissed down my stomach and stopped at my shorts. "I do like these little one. You should wear them all the time." He murmured to me as he pulled them off. Inhaling me, his mouth was on my opening before I knew what was happening. "I have never smelled something so amazing." He said as he kissed my thighs. As soon as his amazing lips touched my sex, his tongue devoured me like I was his last meal.

As he pushed a finger slowly in and out, I moaned, "Logan..." My moans made him growl and the vibrations from his growling only made me moan louder. "Oh god... I'm going to..." he grabbed my behind, lifting me closer to him making his tongue press further and harder until I finally exploded in ecstasy. He didn't miss a beat; he licked every last drop of my juices before putting me back down and kissing me again. I became obsessed with the taste of him and me in his mouth.

"Don't worry little one, we are far from finished." He whispered in my ear.

Making my whole-body shiver.

I watched as he stood and removed his shorts, just staring at this gorgeous god in front of me. My god, perfect doesn't do him justice. His chest was rock solid, and as my eyes fell south, I saw he was so thick and long. My eyes travelled up and down his eleven inches. Was that going to fit in me?

"See something you like little one?" he smirked at me.

I couldn't help the blush that fell over my cheeks. He laid back onto me propping himself up with his elbows. I could feel his erection pressing against my entrance.

"You sure you're ready little one? I'll go slow but it's going to hurt at first but then it will feel a lot better I promise." He was staring into my eyes with so much love I thought I was going to melt.

"I'm ready." And with that he pushed himself slowly in until he was fully inside me. He stayed like that for a minute allowing me to get used to his size. I have never felt so full that it was painful, but there was also a little pleasure mixed in. It only took a couple of good thrusts for the pain to go away and be replaced by extreme pleasure. Logan lowered his head to my neck as he continued his slow deep thrusts. "I love you so much, baby." He said as he moved his head to the crook of my neck and started to grind a little harder and deeper.

"Does it still hurt?" he asked.

"No, it feels damn good. Please don't stop."

He growled in my ear and licked the length of my neck, sending a shiver down my spine.

"Do you want me to go faster?"

"Yes. Faster and harder."

He positioned his arms under my back grabbing my shoulders to hold me in place.

"Tell me if it hurts."

And with that he stopped making gently love to me and started fucking me. His thrusts were so powerful that I was struggling to keep up. My body felt like mush.

Although my vaginal walls were taking a beating, I didn't care because I was in heaven.

As he thrust in and out of me, I was moaning loudly. I was being torn in half and I loved it.

I felt my insides tighten and I knew I was close. He could feel it too. He brought his head down to my neck again and I could feel his teeth grace my shoulder in a questioning way.

"Yes, Mark me Logan now."

While I was experiencing an orgasm, he bit down on my shoulder and it made it stronger and last longer. As my muscles clenched, I felt his seed fill me up. And still, he keeps pumping into me.

"You. Are. Mine" he growled in my ear.

"Yes, I am yours forever."

Finally, his body slowed, and he collapsed on top of me.

When we could finally breathe again, he pushed himself up and looked at me.

"I didn't hurt you did I baby?"

"Not in a bad way."

"Good, now let's get you some of those chocolates."

I love this man... he was damn perfect.

"I love you, that sounds perfect."

He stood up and helped me off the bed.
"I'm going to grab a quick shower, want to join me handsome?"
He growls "You don't have to ask me twice."

Chapter 15

Unknown POV

I watched them enter the little café, laughing to myself as I saw her shift uncomfortably under my gaze. If I didn't know better, I would swear she knew I was watching her. But I knew the truth she had no idea I had finally found her. It took me ten years to find the little she-wolf, but this time she won't escape me.

Watching her today only fuelled my anger; she has taken everything from me, and I will take everything from her.

Today though I'll hold myself back, I want to take my time with her. I want to enjoy her pain.

Andy POV

The café was just as beautiful as I thought it would be, everything was so cute, from the white old-fashioned chairs to the purple flowers that hung down over the balcony.

I am not going to lie, this place was my heaven, adorable and filled with chocolate. I felt at ease here, but something was making me feel uncomfortable. If I didn't know any better, I would think somebody was watching me.

"Are you okay little one?" Logan asked.

"I'm okay handsome, I just had a strange feeling like someone was watching me."

"You probably feel like that because I am always watching you." He whispered next to my ear. His breath tickled my neck making me shiver.

"You're always watching?"

"Of course, I am, little one. I enjoy the view." He sent me a subtle wink as he turned to find us a table.

Following him, I couldn't help but stare at his broad shoulders, I could see every muscle line running down his shoulders and connecting to his arms. He was a work of art sculpted by an artist. The details of his body were flawless and just made me fall in love with him more.

I have never been like this before; I swear I'm going to attack this man when we get home. All I can think about is running my hands down his chest until I got to his...

What's wrong with me?

Nothing is wrong with you Doll, you are just eyeing up our mate and trust me you`re not the only one. My wolf purred in my head.

But I can't keep drooling over him in public.

Then close your mouth, or better yet fill it with him.

I couldn't stop the small moan that slipped through my lips making my cheeks burn from the blush that filled them.

You are such a slut... I yelled at my wolf.

We share a mind Doll, and you are just as bad as I am. The only difference is that I speak my mind.

"What are you doing little one?" The laughter in Logan's voice was apparent, but he was trying hard not to let it out.
"My wolf is being stupid."

You little liar! How dare you, you agree with everything I sa...
I blocked her before she could finish. I didn't want to argue with her. Mainly because she was right.

"Ok little one lets have some cake." That one lovely word made the stupid argument with my wolf disappear.
I will try every cake...

Chapter 16

Logan POV

Yesterday was amazing, so it was strange to wake up to an empty bed. I tried to figure out why she had left. Having mated and completed our mate bond, I took her to the cafe I told her about. She was so excited it was the most adorable thing I had ever seen. Then she tried to taste every cake they made, she made it to eight before admitting defeat. Having bought her the biggest box of chocolates, she growled at me when I suggested she save some for Lex, mumbling something like "he can buy his own damn chocolates." We spent the evening cuddling up in the common room watching movie after movie.

So why did she leave? I got dressed and went looking for her, it was still early, maybe 5am, but I heard someone singing so I followed the voice. Whoever they were, they sounded beautiful, and their voice immediately made me feel calmer. I walked into the kitchen and saw Andy dancing in a pink apron and singing along with the music. I watched her feel so at home in my house and it filled me with joy. I went to her and wrapped my arms around her waist as I danced with her. She jumped but giggled when she realised it was me.

"I woke up without you little one. I was worried."

"I had to wake up early to make Alexi a cake. He's moving into the pack house today. I have to go home to help him finish packing in a little while." She told me as she kissed my cheek. What did she mean home? She was home, I wanted her to stay here with me. She must have seen the worry in my eyes because she asked.

"Are you okay handsome? You seem sad."

"Can I ask you something Andy?" I asked her nervously. When she nodded, I continued? "would you move in with me? Here in the pack house?" I finished in a rush.

She stopped decorating the cake and turned around to face me, she grabbed my face in her hands bringing me down for a kiss. "Of course, I will handsome."

I was so happy I picked her up and put her on the counter getting between her legs. I kissed her again.

"As tempting as the idea is, I'm not having sex with you in a kitchen." She said as the kiss broke.

"One day little one, you will."

I stayed with her as she finished the cake and helped her clean up when she was finished. I just wanted to spend as much time as I could with her before she left.

"I'm going to get dressed and head to Lex. I won't be gone too long." She kissed me as she left the kitchen. After being away from her for less than two hours, I was unable to focus on anything. In my attempts to find out why Andy shifted so early or how she could have set the building on fire; I contacted our pack elders. All they replied with was that they would look into it. I hated waiting so I tried to distract myself by getting her a gift to celebrate her move in, but I didn't think of anything good. After a sigh, I sat back down at my desk.

Where were they? They must be on their way back by now. How much stuff does the boy own? I tried to get back to work but didn't get much done. Eventually there was a knock on the door, and I heard Alexi's voice.

"Hey dude, you in there?"

I got up and went to open the door and was greeted by a smiling Lex.

"You going to come help her move all this stuff, or am I?"

"I'm coming. Where is she?" I asked as we started walking downstairs.

"She's trying to unpack the car; I keep telling her it's a two-man job and she just glares at me and tries to do it herself grumbling about how she's stronger than any man" he started laughing as we got outside and when I turned, I couldn't help laughing too. She was trying to lift a wardrobe on her own. I think she could have done it if it were not two feet higher than her.

She glared at us, "Why don't you two stop laughing and help?"

Between the three of us we managed to get all of the things in the house rather quickly.

"Thank god that's done." Alexi said as he collapsed on one of the couches.

"Oh, that reminds me I made you a welcome gift." Andy said as she jumped off the couch and ran to the kitchen.

"I don't know how she has so much energy." Alexi grumbled to me.

"It's all the sugar." I answered, making us both laugh.

"What do you think?" Andy asked him as she placed the cake in front of him. The thing was perfect, it was a simple white cake topped with all kinds of sweets and coloured chocolate dripped down the sides.

"It's amazing, little sister, do I smell cherry's?" he asked her, starting to get excited.

She laughed at him and she nodded giving him a knife and a small plate. Andy came back and sat beside me again. She cuddled up to my chest and I wrapped my arms around her.

"You too are way too cute; it makes me feel sick." Alexi started laughing as Andy tried to hit him with a pillow but missed.

We all sat there peacefully chatting away until the omegas came in telling us dinner was ready. Once we were sitting in the dining hall with our food, I couldn't help but watch Andy. I was so lucky to have her, and I was going to make sure she knew it for the rest of her life.

"Hey handsome, what are you thinking about?" she asked, staring at me with her eyes filled with so much love that I couldn't help but smile.

"I was wondering how you became such a good fighter?"

"Our Dad taught me, not long after I moved to the pack some kids beat me up. When I came home covered in blood, he took me outside and said, 'the next time someone hits you, hit them twice as hard' we spend every afternoon for months practicing."

"Why would someone beat you? You were just a kid!" I could feel my wolf getting angry at the thought of someone harming our mate.

She looked down at her hands avoiding my question, so I looked towards Lex.

He sighed but answered. "because Connor is a dick, he and some of his idiot buddies cornered her after school."

"You're right he is a dick; I still don't understand why he hates you so much." I turned to Andy and she just shrugged at me.

"We have to run the pack training tomorrow and I was thinking you could join us?" I asked her. She seemed quiet for a moment but eventually she nodded.

"I don't know how much the pack will appreciate me there, but I'll come."

"You're their Luna, they're going to love you." She smiled up at me before returning to her food. The rest of the day was surprisingly uneventful. We spent most of it curled up on the couch watching a musical that Andy kept humming along to.

When we left for training the next day, I could feel how nervous Andy was and I tried my best to calm her down. Once we began sparring, she relaxed quickly, though, since every wolf who fought Andy lost. It was awe-inspiring to watch her fight, the whole group stopped to watch. I had never seen anyone fight with such strength and elegance at the same time, and I knew my pack felt the same as they cheered her on every time she won a match.

"That was fun." She said running up to me.

"Fun? That was extraordinary, little one." I told her as I wrapped my arms around her.

"Are you coming back to the pack house?"

"I have a meeting in town, but I shouldn't be going too long." She frowned at me, making me chuckle. "I'll bring back chocolates."

"Best mate ever! I love you." She said as she ran back to the house which was over two miles away.

"How does she do that? I'm exhausted just watching her." Alexi said.

"I have no idea, but we better get going if we are going to make it to town." He nodded and followed me.

"She still has no idea why we are really going?" he asked as we drove away.

"Nope. None." I smiled at him.

Chapter 17

Andy POV

I spent all morning nervous about training with the pack, but they were actually nice to me. They asked me to give them lessons, so I agreed, and am teaching training tomorrow... it went better than I expected, and I couldn't be happier. When it ended, I was so full of adrenaline that I decided to run back to the pack house. Alexi and Logan have to go into town for a meeting, so a run will keep me busy. I hated being away from Logan, it was crazy how much I missed him in just a few hours.

Something is following us! My wolf growled in my head.

How do you know?

I can smell them.

It wasn't far. I decided to speed up going as fast as I could towards the pack house. I could see it in the distance, so I pushed harder. I could hear people running on either side of me, they were surrounding me. When I entered the clearing in front of the house, a wolf lunged at me. Before I could shift, I heard a gunshot and felt searing pain shoot through my back as I fell to the ground.

Before the world went black, I heard a voice say, "Got you now, bitch."

"Wake up, bitch." Something hit me across the face... I opened my eyes to see Connor standing in front of me with a smirk on his face. After attempting to grab him, I realized I was tied to a chair with barbed wire. Whenever I attempted to break free, the wire cut into my skin and started to burn, which caused me to whimper in pain.

"We soaked the wire in wolfsbane, so there is no escape. If you try to shift, the wire will cut through you, killing you." He scoffed at me.

After another attempt, the pain was too intense, and I gave up. Connor started laughing at my futile attempts to get free.

He laughed again at me when I replied, "I'll kill you!"

"You're not going to be doing much of anything."

"What do you want with me?"

"What makes you think I want you."

If not me then who? Logan...

"He will kill you. He'll rip you in two." I screamed at him. He just glared at me.

"I'm prepared for that don't worry. He can't kill all of us." Was the last thing he said before he left. I tried to figure out where I was. There wasn't much light, but I could tell the space was tiny, and it smelled like mud and fish. Maybe I was in a fishing cabin. Given that we were in Cornwall, that wasn't very helpful.

Crap.

Logan! Logan! He didn't answer my call.

It's no use Doll, we're covered in wolfsbane. It prevents mind linking. I knew she was right, but it infuriated me.

What are we going to do? I can't break out of this.

You're going to have to use your power again.

Hell no. I can't control it. The last time I tried I burnt down a building...

You were a pup, but you are not a child anymore. Stop fearing what you are.

I don't even know what I am. How can I fear it?

You have not tried to do it again since that night. You have no idea what we are capable of. If you want to save our mate, you have to try.

She was right, I had never tried using it again. The idea scared the hell out of me.

How? What do I do? I pleaded.

Concentrate. You are not just setting buildings ablaze. There is so much more that can be done, just let go.

When I closed my eyes, I concentrated on the heat I felt the day of the fire, but there was no burning sensation and no flames.

It didn't work! I yelled at my wolf.

Keep trying.

So, I did, I kept trying. For hours until I was exhausted but still nothing happened. I couldn't keep my eyes open anymore and I slipped into unconsciousness.

Chapter 18

Logan POV

"Where the hell is, she?" I yelled for the hundredth time. We had gotten home hours ago only to find Andy never arrived. Mind linking isn't working, something is blocking her. Where is my mate...

"We'll find her." Mr Jackson (Andy's father) had been trying to calm me down since he arrived, but it wasn't working. Nothing was.

We were all gathered in my office, trying to find out who the hell took her. I was there with Alexi, my father, and Mr Jackson. All we knew was that she had been abducted before she arrived at the house.

"Sorry Alpha, but I thought you might like to see this." Mr Thompson announced as he entered the room. He is one of the pack elders, specifically the one I assigned to find out about Andy's power.

"Come in. Did you find anything that can help us?" I hoped.

"I'm not sure, I have an idea about what Miss Hale may be, but I need to ask you some questions before I'm sure."

"What questions?"

"Have any of you seen her wolf?" he asked, looking

at all of us.

When we all shook our heads, he looked disappointed but continued. "What about her eyes?"

"Her wolves are bright blue. They almost look like flames." I explained honestly. As I watched the others look confused at our conversation, I realized they had no idea she was different.

"I will say then it's quite possible I am correct, but it's hard to tell for sure without seeing her wolf." Get to the point already. When I just stared at him, he continued.

"There are ancient texts about white wolves. They are extremely rare. There are only a few documented cases in our history. From what you told me; she fits the criteria. They can shift from childhood if they feel threatened. They are also stronger, faster and have more endurance than a regular wolf, but the most extraordinary part is their power. They can control one of the elements, such as earth, fire, water, or air. Their eyes tell you which one they are. He finished with, "Red flame for fire, green leaves for earth, blue waves for water, and grey wind for air."

We all just stared at him confused. Is Andy a white wolf? It would explain the fire but...

"Her eyes are blue, not red. So, what does that mean?" I asked him.

"I'm not sure alpha. It's possible it's just a deformity." He offered.

"Thank you, Thompson." I said dismissing him.

"Have we missed something?" Alexi asked me after Thompson left.

"It's a long story and not mine to tell, but I think he's right. I think Andy might be a white wolf."
"Does that help us find her?" he asked me.
"I have no idea."

Chapter 19
Andy POV

I am not sure how long I have been here. It feels like weeks. I have felt my wolf becoming weaker, and no matter how hard I try, my power is failing me. My closest experience to escape was setting a paper plate on fire. Which confused my kidnappers, luckily, they are not the smartest bunch.

I haven't eaten for days. Every time I move, the wire cuts me even deeper, and the wolfsbane's burning agony causes me to pass out - the weaker I get, the angrier I become.

Since I got here, I haven't seen Connor again. They all seem like they are just waiting for something.

Idiot number one walks through the cabin door saying, "Wake up bitch." Oh yeah idiot number one. I think his real name is Derrick, but the nickname suits him more. He has been the only person I've seen in over a week. He's also disgusting. He enjoys watching me in pain. Every morning he brings me food and eats it in front of me. He's the first person I'm killing the second I get free I decided that the second he put his hands on my chest. Pervert!

"The show's about to start." He says smirking at me.

"What show? What the hell do you want with me?"
"We want you to die."
"Then just kill me!" I scream at him. He starts laughing at me "Believe me I want to, but well someone's paid well to kill you themselves." What? Who? "Who?"
"Me, sweetheart." That voice, I know that voice. I knew that it couldn't be him, but when I saw him, he started walking around like Derrick to get closer to me. He looks older, his hair is starting to turn white, and his face is now wrinkled, but his sneer is still the same.
"Remember me sweetheart?" Taking off his jacket, he pushed his arm toward me. "You're the freak who gave me this." His whole left arm was covered in scars, it looked like the skin had melted off. "You killed my whole unit, sweetheart."
"You killed my family!" I yelled at him as he stepped closer. He tightly grasped my neck, leaving me unable to breathe. As I struggled I felt the wires cut into my skin. My vision began to fade, but before I passed out, he released his grip.
'You don't think I would let you die so easily, do you? I am going to make it hurt, but first let me figure out who you are sweetheart.' He laughed while grabbing something metallic from the floor. As he walked back towards me, I could see it more clearly. It was a crowbar.
"let's have some fun, sweetheart." He smirked at me and struck me with a crowbar, causing my ribs to break.

He said as he hit me again, "We're just getting started, sweetheart." I could hear Derrick laughing as the crowbar collided with my face.

"Is that all you've got arsehole?" I felt my anger rising inside me. It felt like it was burning me from the inside out.

He snarled at me as he grabbed something from his bag. I heard hissing and knew what it was before I saw it.

Putting the blowtorch against my cheek, he sneered and hissed as he spewed fumes at me. I closed my eyes, awaiting pain, but it did not come. I only felt heat. My anger was building, I felt like I was going to explode.

"What the fuck," he yelled at me. As I opened my eyes, I saw why. The flames touched my skin, but instead of burning me, it appeared as if they were attracted to me.

He screamed at me again as he struck my face. The second his fist struck my face, the blowtorch exploded in his hand. I could smell burnt meat as the flames consumed his right arm. He screamed as he attempted to put out the blaze, but nothing worked. I watched it burn until I heard him. Wolves were howling, so close I couldn't believe it. The loudest of the wolves made my body shiver, and I knew it was him.

"LOGAN!" I screamed as loud as I could. So caught up in the howls I didn't notice the flames had evaporated and he was coming back towards me looking ready to kill.

"You stupid freak. Your friends aren't going to help you. We have been waiting for them. Your friends are going to die. Starting with that alpha of yours but don't worry sweetheart you'll be joining them soon enough." He smirked at me as he left. Leaving me alone with Derrick to listen as my family died.

I cannot do this to them. I can't lose another family. I cannot do this to them. They will all die because of me.

Don't worry Doll. My wolf spoke up.

Where have you been? We need to warn them!

I've been waiting for the right time. And we're not going to warn them.

What? But they'll die.

We're not going to warn them. We're going to save them.

How?

Get up! She howled at me.

I tried to break free, but the wires cut me deeper causing me to whimper. Idiot Derrick started laughing as he watched my useless attempts.

Get up! Stop holding it in. Let it out! She howled again.

I did as she said. I released every last ounce of anger that had been burning me up. The wires holding me tight snapped like twigs as I pushed my way through. I could see all of my cuts closing as I stood, but I heard Derrick gasp and turned my head to see him staring at me. It seemed that his eyes were full of hate and fear as the room became brighter. I tried to figure out where it was coming from. A bright blue light engulfed the small room, but it didn't hurt my eyes like it should have. Since I'm a wolf, I have enhanced senses. Any light this bright should hurt, but it didn't, it was beautiful. After looking down, I realized that all of me was glowing. I heard bones cracking and realised that Derrick had shifted and was coming towards me. I instinctively threw my hands at him, and he froze. He literally froze. His wolf resembled a block of ice. His paws were off the floor and his mouth was open, exposing his canine teeth.

I stood there in shock, staring at him.

I told you Doll. We are more powerful than you know.

After hearing the fighting start, I didn't have time to reply. Wolves were growling, guns were firing. The chaos I saw made me freeze. Our pack had been trying to attack the hunters and rogues, but they were surrounded. Alexi's light brown wolf was fighting off three rogues. I could tell he was winning but the wolves managed to rip out a chunk from his hind leg. Alexi started to lose his balance when a rogue leapt on him, but before he could finish they were attacked by a massive black wolf, knocking the rogue off.

Black wolf pinned the rogue and became distracted by him, so he did not notice the hunter pointing a gun at his head. Before the hunter could pull the trigger, I growled at him. I swear the earth shook from the force of that growl. The hunter pulled the trigger, but the shaking caused him to miss the wolf. When the black wolf glanced up at me, his emerald eyes locked with mine and for the second time it seemed as if the rest of the world had melted away leaving just us. When I heard the hunter loading his gun again, I was jolted out of our bubble.

He was going to shoot my mate!

In a flash, my wolf took over my body and attacked the hunter without my control. Although he tried to fight back, he was no match for my wolf, which was too big and too strong. I felt something brush against my side causing me to growl until I felt sparks shooting across my skin and I knew it was Logan. I instantly calmed and turned to him.

I've missed you little one. He mind linked me.

I've missed you too handsome.

It wasn't until I faced him that I realized how big my wolf was. I hadn't shifted much and never with anyone. I always thought my wolf would just make me more of a freak. His wolf was 6 feet tall on four legs, but mine was a foot higher than his, although instead of muscle, mine was thinner and more feminine. My pure white fur and blue eyes contrasted perfectly with his pure black fur and green eyes. It was like we were the exact opposite. We completed each other.

More gun shots from the hunters jolted me from my

inner monologue. The fight wasn't over yet.

Chapter 20

Logan POV

I have been without my mate for two weeks. We have searched everywhere and have found nothing. I could feel her. She was getting weaker every day. All we knew was that she was still alive. I was unable to link with her; there was something blocking me. I have barely slept, and my anger is starting to boil over. I keep yelling at innocent omegas. I needed my mate. Having only just found her and already losing her, I hurled my plate across the room, shattering it as it collided with the wall.

"We'll run out of plates soon." Alexi said standing at the door.

"I honestly don't care. Have the trackers found anything?"

"No nothing. I just don't understand how she could just disappear" he sat on one of the couches putting his head in his hands. Andy disappearing has taken its toll on him too. His hair was a mess and he looked like he hadn't shaved since she's been gone.

"We have to try something. There has to..." I couldn't finish my sentence because it felt like someone had their hands around my throat. My chest hurt; I was so sure someone was choking me that I fell to my knees, clutching my throat. I could not breathe. I knew something was wrong, but there was nothing. I felt Alexi run over to me.

"Logan? What the hell is happening." He was searching for an injury but couldn't find anything.

"Not me. Andy." I choked out.

He growled beside me, but before he could do anything, the pain stopped.

"It's stopped." I said standing up.

"Is she... is she dead?" He asked. I could see tears forming in his eyes. I shook my head, but before I could respond, Connor ran in.

"We found her!" he yelled at us.

"What where?" we both said in unison. The pain started again only this time it wasn't my throat it was my chest. It felt like someone had punched me. I doubled over again but Lex caught me.

"We have to hurry, get the warriors ready now." He yelled as he helped me stand up.

The run to Andy was excruciating. I could feel her pain, not just physical but emotional. Someone was torturing my mate! And I was going to kill them!

We're close. Connor linked us.

Her anger made me feel like I was on fire. My chest grew so hot, yet strangely it wasn't painful. I could feel the heat as though I were on fire myself. It felt like I was going to explode. My wolf howled out from the sensation. All the warriors around me howled too. They wanted their Luna back almost as much as I did. Almost. The burning stopped instantly, and I was worried for a second, but I could still feel her. She was still alive and painfully close.

Before we could break out from the trees into the clearing we were surrounded.

Rogues lined the clearing snarling at us, and humans circled behind us guns in hand.

Humans??

Hunters! My wolf growled at me.

I went for the closest rogue, snapping its neck easily. I kept fighting off every rogue or hunter who came near me. No-one is keeping me from my mate! I caught sight of Alexi in the corner of my eye. He was being pinned down. The filthy rogue was about to snap his neck, so I lunged for him. He tried to fight back but it was useless. I was almost twice his size. I finally had him pinned when I heard her.

She was growling. I swear I saw almost every wolf in the clearing flinched back but not me. She could never scare me. I looked up just in time to see the hunter shoot at me and miss. I found her instantly. The world faded away as I looked into those blue flamed eyes I loved so much. She growled again and I saw the hunter aim for me a second time but before I could move Andy shifted and lunged at him.

Her wolf was beautiful. She was pure white it looked almost like she was glowing. I quickly snapped the rogue's neck and ran towards her. I brushed my muzzle against her side. I felt her tense up but as soon as she realised it was me, she relaxed.

I've missed you little one. I mind linked her.

I've missed you too handsome.

God how much I've missed that voice. When she was facing me, I realised her wolf was massive. Bigger than mine. Her white fur was amazingly soft as it brushed up against my skin. I growled when she moved away. She looked back at me and smiled.
Don't worry handsome I'm not going anywhere but we have a fight to win. She linked at me.
I could feel her giggling at me because I had completely forgotten about the world around us. We went and fought with our pack.

After almost all the rogues were dead, Me, Alexi, Connor, and Andy all stood leading our group when a hunter started laughing... in the middle of a battle he just walked out laughing.
I could see bandages covering his arm and he smelt like burnt meat. He was just staring at Andy with a smirk on his face. I felt Andy tense beside me.
"So that's what you are sweetheart." He started laughing again.
I growled at him.
"I take it, that's the mate. He looks rather ordinary compared to you." I'm going to kill him.
When I lunged at him, I was hit before I could reach him. I looked up and saw Connor standing above me. His grey wolf smiled...
I was so shocked I didn't see Andy knock him off of me. She was circling with him daring him to attack

her.

Chapter 21

Andy POV

I tensed up the moment he walked out into the clearing. He was laughing...
This guy is crazy! What the hell is wrong with him?
"So, that's what you are sweetheart." He started laughing again.
Logan growled at him.
"That must be the mate. He looks rather ordinary compared to you." I growled at him.

How dare he insult our mate!!! My wolf yelled.

Then Logan lunged at him, but before he could reach him, another wolf had jumped on top of him. Although not as big as Logan, the wolf was still pretty big. His appearance was rather plain. A grey wolf. The wolf jumped off my mate as I lunged at it. I circled him, waiting for him to move. I swear if he weren't in his wolf form, he would be laughing... he was enjoying this.

You can't cheat this time! Freak! He mind linked me.

Connor!!! Why was he fighting with us? He jumped at me before I had a chance to reply. As he knocked me down, he bit my hind leg, causing me to howl in pain. Although he went for my throat, I avoided his teeth from puncturing the skin. I growled at him as I bit down on his front paw while clawing at his back. Before I heard him whimper, I felt the bone snap in my mouth. I shook my head, tearing part of his leg as I released him.

As soon as I was off of him, I saw Logan and Alexi jump on him. They kept him down while two of our wolves shifted into human forms before grabbing a bleeding Connor and carrying him away.

They're taking him back. He will pay for his actions. Alexi mind linked.

I just nodded at him; my eyes glued to the hunter who was just watching us. When he walked up to me, he smiled. I glanced down at him, he was at least six feet tall, but my wolf was taller.

"Now we know what you are, we have no use for you." He said as he nodded to his men. I hadn't noticed that so many hunters had entered the clearing. There must have been dozens of them, all carrying large guns. I jumped in front of Logan and Alexi before they could fire. I heard the shots echo in the clearing. I was going to die.

My mate is going to die.

My brother is going to die.

I was so lost in my thoughts that I didn't notice everyone was silent. The wolves and the hunters were frozen in shock. As soon as I opened my eyes, the blue light shone brighter than before, like the

sun had just appeared in my hands. The moment I tore my eyes from them, I noticed a wall between us and the hunters. It looked like a waterfall suspended in mid-air. The water was so still and clear I could see right through it. All the bullets were stuck in it like jelly.
What the hell?

Little one? How'd you do that? Logan mind linked.

I have no idea. I replied honestly.

After realizing my hands were glowing, I was pulled from my thoughts... not paws! Hands! I had shifted! Great... I'm naked in front of a field of men... and my brother...
Why does this stuff happen to me? Logan sensed my panic and walked away...
Soon after, I felt warm hands on my shoulders. I knew it was Logan from the sparks that went down my arms. Taking the t-shirt, he handed me, I quickly changed into it and realized all the wolves were averting their eyes. I need to remember to thank Logan later since I know he must have told them all to look away. By 'told' I mean threaten let's be honest.
On me, the shirt was huge, reaching my knees.
As I looked up, I saw dozens of hunter's yelling at each other, their hatred for us making me shiver.
"Shoot the blonde!" he shouted to his hunters. It took me a second to realize he was talking about me.
It seemed as if the water was fading in front of us. It

was getting smaller and smaller...
What's happening?

We're getting weaker. My wolf answered me.

What do you mean weaker?

Doll, I am exhausted after spending so long here. I have tried to conserve as much energy as possible, but I'm too tired.

It was like my muscles were getting heavier and heavier. Crap, she was right.

"What's happening little one?" Logan asked me.
"I'm getting tired, I can't hold it for too much longer." I felt his arms go around me. I allowed myself to lean on him, trying to steady myself. I could feel my mind fading, the world going black as I fell into Logan's arms.

Chapter 22

Logan POV

When Andy fell limp in my arms, I could sense her exhaustion; saving my family from the hunters was simply too much for her. When she closed her eyes, I saw the wall of protection in front of us fade completely. As I was worried about my mate, I only vaguely noticed all the hunters aiming their weapons again.

Is she okay? Alexi linked me.

I looked up at his golden wolf and nodded my head. "She's okay, she's just exhausted."

Jackson knelt beside me and said, "Give her to me, Alpha. I'll make sure she's safe." He had shifted into his human form and reached out his hands for her. I didn't want to leave my mate; I only just got her back.

We must win a war Alpha, and we need you to do it. Alexi urged me.

Then I nodded and handed my mate over to her father and watched as he carried her away from the fighting.

The hunters tried to shoot my wolves, but my warriors were faster than their aim. I shifted and ran with Lex towards the hunters.

It took a long time, but we finally won, most of the hunters had been killed or wounded. After we had defeated the last hunter, I turned to my wolves, we had lost a lot. We were trying to get everyone back to the pack hospital when I realized one of the hunters was missing. His body wasn't in the field.

"Where is he?" I asked my pack as I searched for his body.

"Who's missing?" Alexi asked me.

"The leader. The one covered in scars. I can't see him." I saw the worry in his eyes as he realized that I was right. He wasn't here. We were the only two who remained as the wolves took the wounded to the pack.

Before I could react, the hunter pointed his gun at me and fired.

There was no blood, no wound, just pain. How was that possible?

"No!" I heard Alexi cry behind me, but I took no notice. All I could think about was the pain radiating from my chest.

I looked up and I understood. Andy was standing in front of me.

When she fell into my arms, I put my arm on her shoulder and asked: "Little one? Are you okay?"

"I'm sorry handsome, I wasn't fast enough." She

whispered as her body fell limp in my arms. The bullet had struck her in the stomach. There was blood everywhere.

"Andy? Andy, please wake up! Please" I begged as I held her in my arms.

"Take her to the hospital now!" I ordered Alexi. He took her from me, and I leapt at the hunter, tearing at him with all the anger that was building in me. He shot her. He shot my mate. The more I clawed at him, the angrier I became.

"Alpha! He's dead." Jackson yelled trying to pull me off him.

"Stop. You have to stop." I ignored him.

"Andrea needs you." That made me pause, and I looked at him. He was right, my mate was dying, and she needed me.

Andy has been treated in the hospital for weeks now. The doctors said that she was in a coma and that they thought she might never wake up. They are wrong, they must be wrong. I will not lose her. Not having her curled up beside me was breaking me. Despite the efforts of my parents, Alexi, and the rest of the pack, I can't leave this hospital room. I won't leave until she does. I won't go home without her.

Chapter 23

Andy POV

The world was pitch black; I couldn't see anything. I tried to get up, but I was stuck, I couldn't move. As soon as I heard his voice, I stopped panicking.

"I'm not going anywhere Alexi" he said, sounding exhausted and defeated. The only thing I wanted to do was reach out and touch him.

"You've been here for weeks. You need to go home!" Alexi argued.

"Enough! I won't leave her." I knew Logan had used his Alpha voice when I felt the power coursing through the room.

"Fine," Alexi mumbled as he left.

Logan held my hand as he said, "I love you little one. Please don't leave me."

"I'm not going anywhere, handsome." I whispered, my voice rough and the words painful, but the smile Logan gave me was worth the pain.

When he kissed me, he said, "You really need to stop doing this to me, little one."

I heard the door open and felt Alexi put his arms around me.

"I thought you were dead, little sister." I could feel

his tears on the back of my neck.

"It takes more than a silver bullet to kill me." I told him as I hugged him back tighter.

The doctors were genuinely surprised when I recovered. They had believed I was as good as dead. It took days before they released me from the hospital after running every test they could.

When they finally let me go, Logan wouldn't let me be on my own. I'm pretty sure he was worried I would break. Pulling into the driveway of the pack house, I began to feel much better.

Logan stopped me when I tried to walk upstairs to our room.

"I have a surprise for you little one," he said as he led me towards the back of the house. We finally stopped outside of a simple wooden door. I stared at Logan waiting for him to explain but he just opened the door.

"Do you like it?" he asked nervously. I couldn't form the words, I was so shocked. The room was painted a beautiful shade of red, and in the middle of it stood a massive white grand piano. It looked just like my mothers.

"It's amazing. My mother had one just like it." I said as I walked towards the piano.

"Not like it, little one. It's hers."

"What? How? I thought it was destroyed in the fire?" I asked confused.

"It was damaged but not destroyed, but Jackson kept it and some of their things in storage. When Alexi told me about it, I had it repaired for you."

I stared at him with tears streaming down my face, and between sobs I said, "Thank you Logan. I love you."

"I love you too little one."

He is my mate, and I am blessed to have this house and family. I had finally arrived home. I had been freed from Connor and the hunters who had killed my family. I still missed my parents, but I was so grateful to have Alexi and my family here with me and for Logan. Finally, I felt at home, like I belonged somewhere.

Finally, my life was beginning, and I couldn't wait to see where it would take me next.

To be continued in book 2...

Chapter 1
Andy's POV

So, my life somehow got so much better...

The worst experience in my life was when my mate rejected me when I turned 18, but that led me to Logan, the sweetest man I've ever met. It was as if the Goddess apologised for making me deal with Connor by making Logan my second chance mate!

Connor being the dick he is, started working with the most horrendous man on the planet. A hunter... he killed my whole pack when I was younger, I was the only survivor. I had no idea he had survived the attack until he kidnapped me...

You heard me right, he kidnapped me, and Connor helped him hold me for weeks.

Despite their efforts to bring me home, Logan and Alexi were too late. I was severely injured and no longer able to heal. Doctors said I was in a coma and would never wake up. However, once again the Goddess was on our side, because despite all odds I awoke.

That's my story, or the short version anyway. So here I am settling into my reading chair at the pack house, my handsome mate fast asleep on the bed in front of me. Everything crazy I have experienced over the past two months has been worth it, because I will spend the rest of my life with him.

Until two months ago, all I wanted to do was run away from this pack; now the idea of leaving is horrible. This pack is my home, it is perfect, and I have everything I could ever want.

"Good morning, little one. What are you doing up so early?"

When I first saw Logan, I couldn't help but stare at him shirtless as he sat there, staring at me with his cheeky grin. I couldn't stop my eyes from drifting downwards, his eight pack in full view.

When I finally stopped eye fucking my mate, I noticed a smirk playing across his lips, obviously enjoying the attention.

"I couldn't sleep."

A look of concern crossed his face as he crossed the room towards me, wrapping his arms around me. The feeling of being in my mates arms instantly started calming me.

"What's wrong, Love?"

My stomach ache disappeared as he smiled at me. "Nothing, I'm fine. It's been a crazy couple of months. Besides, today I officially become Luna. I don't care for parties or being in the centre of attention."

As he spoke, his expression relaxed: "You don't have to worry, they'll adore you. You were born to lead. Come on, let's get ready and then have breakfast, I asked the omegas to make pancakes."

Goddess I love this man, he truly knows the way to

my heart. Smiling from ear to ear as I followed him to the bathroom, to shower with my beast of a mate. Sometimes I really do love my life.

It took an hour for us to finally make it to the dining room, seeing Logan soaped up in all his glory was just plain distracting. It would be impossible to look at Logan Black, 6 feet of unrelenting muscle, and not be distracted. That man is intoxicating, whenever he is around it's like my brain is clouded in fog.

I was getting used to living in the pack house, even getting into a routine. Alexi and I trained the warriors in the morning, then I spend the afternoon taking care of pack business. It was a simple routine, but I had grown to love it, however today's different. This is the first full moon I have seen since I became Logan's mate, that is, the first one during which I have actually been here. Kidnapping and Coma not included. Meaning today is my Luna ceremony, the day I officially become Blue Moon's Luna. I'm terrified, this pack has avoided me for years, most of them have pretended like I don't exist since I moved here. Training with the warriors over the past couple of weeks has been incredible but I'm still nervous. I haven't spent a lot of time with the rest of the pack, so i have no idea how they're going to react to me. Logan keeps saying they will love me; I just wish I were as confident as he is.

An Omega pulled me from my inner monologue, as she placed a plate of chocolate chip pancakes in front of me. "Morning Luna."

"Morning Megan, these look amazing. Thank you."

She smiled proudly before heading back to the kitchen, I liked Megan. She is very timid and quiet, but rather sweet. Her short hair was cut into a bob that brushed against her bare caramel skin. Her father is one of the warriors I trained, so when he said she wanted a summer job, I offered her a job in the pack house. Despite my repeated attempts to get her to call me Andy, she still calls me Luna.

"Morning guys. Andy you missed a crazy training session."

As I looked at Alexi, he was sweaty and smelled of death. The house is overrun with boys, I can't wait until Grayson and Alexi find their mates. I'm outnumbered here.

"You stink!"

He rolled his eyes at me but continued his story. "So Gray goes mad on Damon and destroys him, not that he didn't have it coming, the guy is a tool."

That's an understatement, Damon was Connor's closest friend and just as evil as him. He hated me, well, still hates me. He refuses to even acknowledge that I am there, he is one of the warriors and will not take a single order from me. Alexi wants him punished, but I refuse; if Logan found out, I think he would lock him up with Connor.

"You talking about me behind my back again, Lex?" Grayson jokingly asked as he entered, sporting exactly the same post exercise look like Alexi. With his stormy grey eyes, black hair that was reminiscent of beautiful silk and his adorable smile, he was one of the most eligible bachelors in the pack. Standing in nothing but grey sweatpants, I could almost hear every woman in the pack house swoon.

As Logan growled beside me, I realized I had been gazing at the gamma for far too long. Alexi laughed at Grayson's discomfort, seeing that Logan looked like he might kill him.

"You have nothing to worry about handsome."

Logan visibly relaxed at my voice, still glaring at Grayson as he pulled me on to his lap.

Away from my pancakes...

My efforts to move away towards my food only angered my mate, mainly because Grayson had chosen to sit beside me. Goddess why is he so big, I can barely move him!

Alexi was laughing at my struggle, damn traitor. Just sitting there as I starve to death. My glaring only made him laugh harder, and he calls himself my brother.

"You could help me, you know?" I all but sneered at my brother.

"I could." He agreed.

I'm going to wipe that smug smile off of his stupid face as soon as I'm free. I heard Grayson laugh as he realised what was happening, a growl slipped from my lips, instantly silencing the wolf.

"Never get between Andy and food, trust me dude."

Grayson seemed to accept this and went back to his pancakes.

"Handsome, can you please let me go?" Logan gave me a confused look before releasing me from his death grip.

I took one bite of my breakfast before Megan walked in and announced "Luna, it's time to get ready for the ceremony." With one last mournful look at my food, I stood and followed her upstairs.

In addition to planning the whole ceremony, Logan's mother, the former Luna, even picked out my dress, which I have to admit is stunning. A simple red one shoulder ball gown, it fit me perfectly. My height made it just reach the floor, allowing it to flow behind me as I walked.

Megan had been assigned to do my hair and makeup, after two hours of sitting in the chair with her fussing over me I realised why Luna had picked her. The girl was talented, I can't believe she made me look so elegant. My makeup wasn't over the top, but it was still stunning. The sides of my hair were swirled into a braid, that laid on top of my tamed curls. I don't think I have ever looked so put together before, don't get me wrong I dress up sometimes but nothing like this, nothing so elegant. Smiling from ear to ear I hugged Megan, thanking her.

"You're coming right? Please say yes, I could use a friend." I begged.

"I do not think I was invited; besides, I do not have anything to wear."

"Don't worry, we can fix that."

About The Author

Alexa Phoenix

Alexa Phoenix writes sweet, fun, action-packed fantasy. Her characters are clever, fearless, and adventurous but in real life, Alexa spends all of her time curled up with a book in her hands, daydreaming. Let's face it. Alexa wouldn't last five minutes in one of her books.

If you liked the book, please leave a review.

Follow her on Facebook: AlexaPhoenixFantasyWriter

Books By This Author

Rejecting The Alpha

Amelia

Life has a funny habit of throwing the most peculiar curveballs at you.
Up until now I thought my life was fairly ordinary, but I was so wrong.
After losing my parents two years ago, I found it hard to believe in anything.
Then I met him… Oscar Campbell.
He has changed my entire perspective on life and the world around me. The supernatural world exists and it's closer than any of us realize.
Oscar has awakened something inside of me that I didn't know was there.
I just don't know if I'm ready for this new life.

Made in the USA
Coppell, TX
11 July 2023